# SHERLOCK BONES

## AND THE CURSE OF THE PHARAOH'S MASK

Published in Great Britain in 2022 by Buster Books,
an imprint of Michael O'Mara Books Limited,
9 Lion Yard, Tremadoc Road, London SW4 7NQ

**W** www.mombooks.com/buster

**f** Buster Books

**y** @BusterBooks

**O** @buster_books

A CIP catalogue record for this book is available from the British Library.

ISBN: 978-1-78055-751-9

3 5 7 9 10 8 6 4 2

This product is made of material from well-managed, FSC®-certified
forests and other controlled sources. The manufacturing processes
conform to the environmental regulations of the country of origin.

Printed and bound in December 2023 by
CPI Group (UK) Ltd, Croydon, CR0 4YY.

# SHERLOCK BONES
# AND THE CURSE OF
# THE PHARAOH'S MASK

Written by Tim Collins
Illustrated by John Bigwood

BUSTER BOOKS

**Edited by Frances Evans**
**Designed by Derrian Bradder**
**Cover design by John Bigwood**

# Welcome

Sherlock Bones and Dr Jane Catson are world-famous for solving crimes. Each case is written down by Catson, so you can read all about their adventures.

## Sherlock Bones

Sherlock Bones is the greatest detective the world has ever known. He never runs away from a puzzle, and always cracks his cases.

## Dr Jane Catson

Dr Jane Catson is Sherlock Bones' crime-fighting partner. She's always ready to pounce into action when faced with a sneaky criminal.

Are you ready to help Bones and Catson solve their trickiest case yet? Throughout the story, you will find puzzles where you can put your detective skills to the test. If you get stuck, you can find all the answers at the back of the book, starting on page 169. You can also just enjoy reading the adventure and come back to the puzzles later if you want to. Good luck!

# Chapter One

Where on earth was Hastings? My old friend had said he'd meet us outside the café in the market square, but there was no sign of him.

I could see hundreds of cats crowding around the food stalls, but none of them looked anything like him. I wondered if I'd even recognize him after so much time.

I hadn't seen Hastings since he'd moved to Egypt to set up an antique shop ten years ago. I'd written to him as soon as Sherlock Bones and I booked our holiday to El Kitten, a large city on the River Nile, and I'd been delighted when he'd replied and told us where to meet him.

But he didn't seem to be around. Had I got the time wrong?

Bones was standing next to me with his paws folded.

"He's got to be here somewhere," I said, "Keep your eyes peeled."

I lifed my paw to shield my face from the bright sun and looked around.

"My eyes are always peeled, Catson," said Bones. "I miss nothing. Do you notice that jackal?"

He pointed to an animal approaching a nearby fruit stall. "I can tell from the smooth patches of fur under her eyes that she usually wears glasses, yet she has none today. I think she's forgotten them, and I doubt it will end well."

A moment later, the jackal crashed into the stall, sending oranges and apples tumbling on to the ground. The zebra running the stall scowled at her.

"Told you," he said.

I sighed. Bones is the greatest detective in the world, and loves spotting clues. But I was hoping he'd give it a rest while we were on holiday.

"Very impressive," I said. "But I need you to look for Hastings. My fur was much longer the last time we met, so he might walk straight past me."

"In that case, you should probably look to your left," said Bones. "There's a cat in a white suit that looks like it was made by the tailors Barkley's of London. No doubt he lived in our great city once."

Can you help Catson spot Hastings in the crowd? He's the only cat wearing a plain white jacket.

I turned around. Hastings was indeed waiting nearby. His fur was greyer and his cheeks were plumper, but he was still the same cat I'd sat next to in feline history lessons. He was wearing a gold medallion with a cat's eye on it, and it flashed in the sunshine as he walked over.

"Hastings!" I cried.

"Catson! You haven't changed a bit!" he said in his loud, deep voice, pulling me into a hug. His medallion pressed into my chest.

He released me, and grabbed Bones' paw.

"And you must be Jane's famous friend," he said. "News of your talent has reached this part of the world, believe it or not. We get copies of *The Morning Terrier* here, eventually."

"A publication fit to line any litter tray," said Bones.

There were large tables outside the café that were shaded by wide, white parasols. Hastings guided us to one and clicked his fingers. A gazelle waiter rushed over, followed by three meerkat assistants. He poured glasses of water for us, while the meerkats lined up behind him.

"Afternoon, Ibby," said Hastings. "We'll have the extra-large platter."

The waiter scribbled it down on his pad and trotted away, with his assistants following.

I glugged the water down. I was so hot, it felt as though steam should be shooting out of my ears and nostrils.

"So, how are you finding life in El Kitten?" I asked.

Hastings gestured to the packed square in front of us. Donkeys, impalas and okapi were thudding around, while dogs in white shorts and cats in black robes weaved between them.

"I'm surprised you need to ask," he said. "Look at all the life in this city. You can never be bored. And we have this amazing weather all year."

I could see why my friend liked it so much. Back home, I could wait weeks for a patch of sunlight worth stretching out in. Here, I could do it every day.

"Plus, I enjoy working with antiques," said Hastings. He smiled and leaned back in his chair. "I seem to have a talent for finding ancient and valuable items."

The waiter reappeared and laid our table with plates of hot food while his staff scurried around behind him.

"Eat!" said Hastings. "Enjoy! This is one of the finest restaurants in our town."

I spooned some of the catfood couscous on to my plate and tried it. The blend of tuna chunks, jelly and chopped chillies was delicious, but it soon made the inside of my mouth as hot as the rest of me.

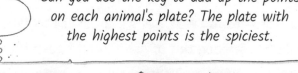

Can you use the key to add up the points on each animal's plate? The plate with the highest points is the spiciest.

1 point  2 points  3 points  4 points  5 points  6 points  7 points

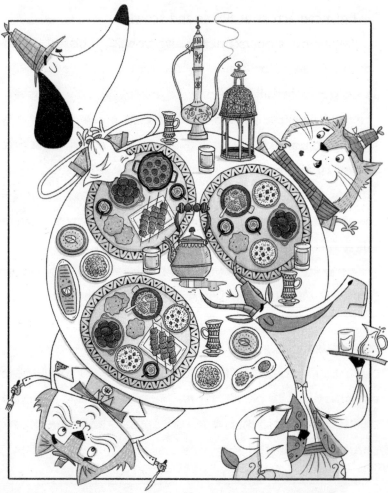

12

Bones smeared some chunks of grilled chicken and onion over a piece of flatbread and took a bite.

He peered at Hastings. "Your arms seem very strong for an antiques dealer. It looks as though you've sharpened your claws. And there are some specks of gold paint on the ends of them."

I glanced across at Bones and scowled.

"Will you stop examining everyone?" I hissed. "We're meant to be on holiday."

Hastings let out a deep laugh and banged the table with his paw. Our plates almost bounced off.

"Don't worry," he said. "It's my pleasure to see the great Sherlock Bones at work. It's true that I need to keep myself fit for work. I have to lift tables, beds and statues as well as smaller items. And as for my claws, I use them to clean the dust out of precious artefacts."

I tried a few chunks of salmon stew. It was just as tasty and spicy as the other dish.

"But enough about me," said Hastings, turning back to me. "What brings you to our great land?"

"Just a holiday," I said. "Even detectives need a break sometimes."

"Well there's so much to see here," said Hastings, grinning broadly. "I can show you the temples, the swimming pool, the royal scratching posts. Did you know we have the world's largest string museum here? You could spend a whole day in there."

The museum sounded very distracting. I once found a ball of string behind the sofa back home, and it took me eight hours to untangle it.

"I'm afraid we won't have time for any of that," said Bones. "We're boarding a boat on the Nile this evening, and we're off to visit the tomb of King Tutancatmun."

Hastings' mouth drooped into a frown. He fixed his green eyes on Bones.

"If I were you, I would stay well away from there," he warned. "Forget your trip."

I didn't want to be rude to my old friend, but there was no way we were going to cancel. Ever since the ancient tomb and golden mask of the old cat pharaoh had been discovered a few months before, we'd been desperate to take a look.

"We've come a long way to see it," I said. "We can hardly turn back now."

Hastings leaned in towards me.

"In that case, I must tell you the truth," he said. "There is a curse on that place. Anyone who enters the tomb and gazes upon the mask will suffer bad luck . . . forever."

Hastings broke off and glanced from side to side.

"It's even said that the mummy of Tutancatmun will come back to life and get revenge on intruders," he whispered. "Do you really want to take that chance?"

# Chapter Two

I was still worrying about what Hastings had said when we reached the port later that afternoon. Usually, I'd pay no attention to silly stories about ancient curses, but this one had come from a trusted old friend, and it was really getting to me. I kept imagining a cat wrapped in bandages rising from a dusty sarcophagus.

I put my heavy case down and stretched my aching arms. There was a waiting room to our left, a small police station to our right, and a jetty sticking out into the river ahead of us. Our boat was at the end of it.

It was a beautiful vessel, with three levels, a giant paddle wheel at the back and two funnels on top. The lowest deck was taken up with a row of cabins. The second deck had a large covered room with a walkway around it, and the top was a wheelhouse where the captain could steer from.

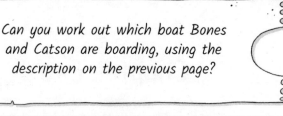

*Can you work out which boat Bones and Catson are boarding, using the description on the previous page?*

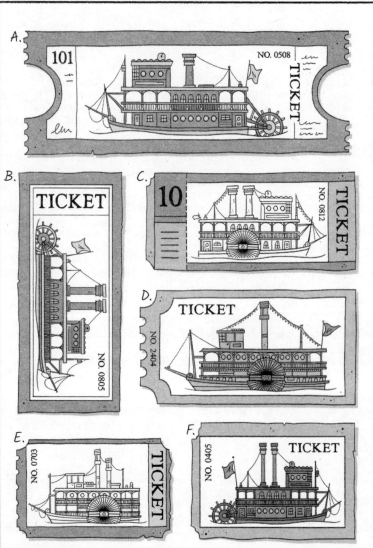

18

"Do you really think we should go?" I asked. "Perhaps we could spend a week exploring the town instead?"

Bones chuckled.

"My dear Doctor Catson," he said. "I do believe your friend has spooked you. And I thought you were such a sensible cat."

"No, it's nothing to do with the curse," I said. "I just thought we should go to the string museum instead. Everyone loves string."

Bones pointed to a queue of animals on the jetty. There was a hippopotamus, a bison, a lion and two pandas.

"Look at all our fellow passengers," he said. "If they're brave enough to take the trip, surely you can be, too?"

The hippopotamus was wearing a fluffy, pink coat, and was surrounded by an eight-piece luggage set. The bison was wearing a tall hat with a wide brim, and standing with his hands on his hips. The lion was wearing a light brown jacket with matching shorts. And the pandas were both wearing straw hats and dark glasses.

They all looked like normal tourists, and not the kind of animals who would set out into real danger.

A camel stepped off the boat and drew the rope aside. She was wearing a dark jacket, and had a satchel over her shoulder.

"Welcome travellers!" she shouted. "I'm Laila, your captain. Please have your tickets ready!"

The hippopotamus stepped forward and shoved her ticket at Laila, who ripped it, and carried two of the hippo's suitcases on to the ship. I think Laila was expecting the hippo to take the rest of the cases herself, but she left them where they were and followed the camel on board.

I had no idea why the hippo would need so many cases. Bones and I had just one suitcase each, for our clothes and books, and small backpacks for day trips. I had my water bottle and emergency cat biscuits in mine, and Bones had his notepad, torch and magnifying glass in his.

The pandas got on next. They said nothing, and barely even looked at Laila as they boarded the ship.

I was beginning to worry that our fellow travellers would all be unfriendly, but the bison boarding next was very talkative. He refused to let Laila carry his bags, and launched into a speech about how long it had taken him to travel to Egypt.

Laila took the lion to his cabin next, and he asked her if the boat had ever sunk, and where the lifejackets were. Finally, she came back for us. We were in cabin four, on the far side of the boat.

The cabin had a small round window. There were two narrow beds along each side, and a writing table opposite the door.

We threw our bags on to the beds, and Laila led us up a set of steps to the second deck, and into the large, covered lounge area that was filled with tables and chairs. A further set of steps at the back led up to the wheelhouse, and there was a tall cupboard to the left of them.

The other passengers were already relaxing on the chairs. They were sipping water from glasses, except for the bison, who was using a golden cup.

We took two seats to the right of the door.

"Off we go!" said Laila. She placed her satchel on top of the cupboard and marched up the stairs. I could hear her pulling some metal levers. Then steam hissed from the stacks high above us and the boat began to chug slowly along the river.

The rest of us stared at each other in silence. I wondered how I could break the ice.

Luckily, the bison did it for me. He leaned over to the pandas, who were sitting next to him and held his hoof out.

"Hi, I'm Teddy, but you probably know me as the Furdryer King," he said. "Started off with one store in

Oklahoma and I now run thirty across the American Mid-West. I can see your fur has good volume, and you're probably happy with your current hair-care regime, but I bet if you gave the new Fur Sonic 5200 a chance, you'd never go back."

One of the pandas took his hoof and gave it a weak shake.

"I'm Annabelle," she said. "And this is my husband, Gerald."

Both pandas then turned away and said nothing more. But their rudeness didn't seem to upset Teddy. He simply moved on to the hippo and started again.

"Now I can see you don't have a lot of fur," said Teddy. "So you might not have much need for my products. But have you ever thought about what perfect gifts they could make for the furry friends in your life? Maybe you're looking for a Christmas present for a cheetah or a birthday present for a mongoose . . ."

"I'm Lady Florence Wallowing," said the hippo. "And I'm too hot. Get me my fan. It's in cabin number one."

Ignoring her request, Teddy moved on to the lion.

"I'm Walter," said the lion. He had a large gold ring, and he twisted it around his finger as he spoke. "But I don't use furdryers because I've heard they can explode and burn your fur."

Study the passengers' passport photos for two minutes, then turn the page to see how much you can remember.

Florence

Teddy

Walter

Annabelle

Gerald

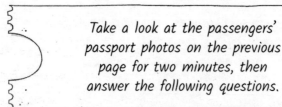

*Take a look at the passengers'
passport photos on the previous
page for two minutes, then
answer the following questions.*

1. How many of the passengers
are wearing hats?

2. Who is wearing a necklace
– Florence or Annabelle?

3. Gerald the panda has a flowery shirt
– true or false?

4. One character has their eyes closed.
Can you name them?

5. Does Walter the lion look
excited or nervous?

6. Which character has a moustache
– Teddy or Gerald?

Teddy launched into a speech about the new safety features of his range before moving on to us. I was waiting for a chance to interrupt him, but he soon interrupted himself.

"Hey, you're Sherlock Bones and Doctor Catson, aren't you?" he asked. "It made the *Oklahoma Times* when you found the Countess of Bitechester's locket. And I should know, because I took out a full-page ad for my No-Tears Junior Furdryer in that very issue."

"A simple case," said Bones. "I'm surprised you found it of interest."

Walter was cowering behind his paws with his mane quivering. He peeked out between his trembling fingers.

"You mean you're detectives?" he asked. "What are you investigating? Are we in any danger?"

Bones laughed.

"Sadly not," he said. "We're just here for a holiday. But if anything happens, we'll be happy to help."

"What sort of thing do you mean?" asked the lion. "Will we be attacked by robbers? Do you think they'll pull our tails?"

I could see the poor fellow was working himself into a state, so I padded over to his seat. Behind me, I could hear Teddy telling Bones about his new range.

"You mustn't worry so much," I said.

The lion was gazing out of the window and taking shallow breaths.

"I'm sorry," he said, eventually. "I'm just a little on edge. When I was staying in El Kitten I overheard a lot of animals saying there was a curse on Tutancatmun's tomb. It frightened me so much that I almost cancelled the trip."

A shiver ran down my spine and tail. Just as I was beginning to forget about the curse, here it was again.

"I've heard all that nonsense, too," I said, trying to sound steady and confident. "Don't listen to a word of it."

The lion gazed at me with wide eyes.

"I tried not to believe it," he said. "But last night I had a dream in which a cat wrapped in bandages rose out of a sarcophagus. It opened its dry throat and told me to stay away."

I felt my fur bristle. This was just the image that had been in my mind all afternoon.

"Just a silly dream," I said. "Nothing bad will happen."

There was a loud bang beneath us, and the ship lurched to a halt. Florence screamed and dropped her glass, which smashed into pieces around her feet.

"The curse!" yelled Walter, cowering behind his paws. "The curse has struck us already!"

# Chapter Three

Laila rushed down from her cabin.

"Sorry, everyone," she said, dashing past us. "Engine problems. I'm sure I'll have it all fixed soon."

Florence pointed to the glass around her feet.

"Clear this up!" she said. "Then get me a grass salad. I'm starving."

Laila ignored her, and shot out through the door at the back of the lounge.

"How rude," said Florence. "Couldn't she hear me?"

She scanned around the room, and fixed her eyes on me.

"You," she said. "Cat. When do we eat?"

"I'm sure it won't be long," I said.

I grabbed Bones and took him back down to our cabin before the hippo could appoint us as her servants.

"Sorry to leave you with that bison," I said. "It sounded like he was talking you through every one of his products."

"I found him rather fascinating," said Bones. "He knows exactly how long it takes the fur of each animal to dry. It's the sort of thing that could turn out to be useful on a case."

I opened my bag and took out my copy of *Meow!* magazine. I couldn't wait to find out what all my favourite celebrities had been up to.

"Try to forget about work," I said, opening my magazine. "Didn't you bring anything to read?"

"Of course," he said.

He unlocked his suitcase and pulled out *The Dictionary of Egyptian Hieroglyphics*, *The Bumper Book of Secret Criminal Societies* and *The Encyclopaedia of Animal Droppings*. None of the books seemed like fun holiday reading.

We went back up the stairs and settled in some deckchairs at the end of the walkway. There were some date palms and low white houses on the shore opposite, with black mountains rising in the distance. A couple of young crocodiles emerged from one of the houses, waving and snapping their teeth at us.

I tried to focus on my celebrity magazine. Apparently, the actress Ginger La Marr had bought a new mansion with fifteen golden cat flaps, and the panda film-star couple Lily Blossom and Wade Power had gone missing from the set of their latest film.

I usually loved this sort of gossip, but I couldn't stop fretting about the curse. Two separate animals had told me about it now. Were we heading straight into the paws of an ancient, undead fiend?

I was glad of the distraction when Teddy clopped over to show us his golden cup. It had pictures of ancient cat kings etched all around it.

"Look what I picked up in El Kitten," he said. "It's a genuine drinking vessel from the days of Tutancatmun. Now, how much do you think I paid for it?"

Bones took out his magnifying glass and peered at it.

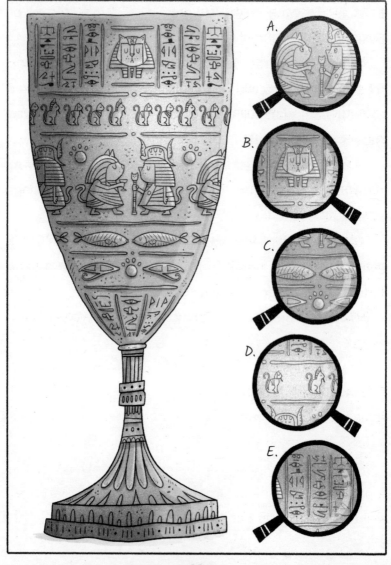

"Let me see," he muttered. "It has straight edges and an even base. It's covered with gold paint and those pictures were carved out with a sharp claw just a few days ago. I would guess that whoever sold it to you said it was worth over a thousand Egyptian pounds, but let you have it for fifty."

"Speak up," said Teddy, cradling his ear. "I can't hear you."

I glared at Bones, and he put his magnifying glass away.

"A thousand Egyptian pounds," I said. "We can't believe you paid less than that for it."

"Wrong," said Teddy. "I paid just fifty. You're right that it's worth a cool thousand, though. But if anyone knows how to make a deal, it's me."

Teddy lifted up the cup and the slanting rays of the sun caught its surface. Fake or not, it looked rather beautiful, and I was glad he was pleased with it.

"Did you buy it from an antiques dealer called Hastings, by any chance?" asked Bones.

"That was the guy," said Teddy. "How did you know?"

"I met him earlier today," muttered Bones. "And I noticed some specks of fresh gold paint on his claws."

Teddy looked puzzled.

"He's an old friend of mine," I said, stamping on Bones' foot. "He's the best antiques dealer in the country. You did well to get a bargain out of him."

Teddy grinned, and moved on to show his cup to Annabelle and Gerald, who were sitting on the other side of the deck. The pandas ignored him, and refused to guess how much he'd spent.

"I can see how your friend has been so successful," said Bones. "Every time a rich tourist comes along, he discovers another 'priceless' artefact in his workshop."

It was a shame to discover that Hastings had been tricking travellers. Looking back, he hadn't always been the best-behaved cat at school. He would often distract teachers in lessons by moving the reflection from his watch around the walls, and he once ruined Christmas dinner by putting catnip in the pudding.

"Do you think we should tell the police about him?" I asked.

"I doubt they'd care," said Bones. "They've got bigger problems than a few wealthy tourists paying too much for trinkets."

I was secretly glad we didn't have to report Hastings. I would have felt like a traitor, however crooked his business was.

It was also good to be reminded that he didn't always tell the truth. Perhaps he'd been lying about the curse, too. Perhaps he'd made it all up as a prank.

This put my mind at rest, and I could sit back and enjoy my magazine. Bones seemed to be enjoying his animal droppings encyclopaedia, too. He kept breaking off to sketch different types of poo in his notebook.

"If only I'd had this sooner," he said after a while. "Did you know that the poos of the Bengal cat are thinner and pointier than those of the Persian cat? That could have helped us so much when we were tracking that gang of bank robbers through the Black Forest."

"Will you stop thinking about work?" I asked. "We might not get another holiday for years."

Bones sighed.

"I suppose you're right," he said. "I just don't find anything as exciting as crimes. I wish someone would commit one now to keep me occupied."

"Well, they're not going to," I said. "So relax."

The sound of Teddy screaming rang out from the lounge behind us.

"Help!" he cried. "There's been a terrible crime."

# Chapter Four

Bones dashed into the lounge with his ears up.

"What seems to be the problem?" he asked.

Teddy pointed to a space on the table next to the water jug.

"My golden cup," he said. "I left it here a moment ago, and now it's gone. Someone must have stolen it!"

Bones' ears fell and his shoulders drooped.

"Oh, is that all?" he asked. "Not much of a puzzle. I'll leave you in the capable paws of Doctor Catson here."

He slouched out of the door, and went back outside.

"Well?" asked Teddy. He had his arms folded and was tapping his hoof on the floor.

"Just give me a moment," I said.

Bones had considered the case so easy that it wasn't even worth explaining. So what had happened?

I decided to think my way through the problem, just as Bones would. No one had got on or off the boat since the cup had gone missing. So the thief was on board.

I knew that neither Bones or I had taken it, which left Laila, Walter, Florence, Annabelle and Gerald.

Laila had been busy fixing the engine, and probably knew enough about ancient artefacts to see that the cup was worthless.

Had the lion, the hippo or the pandas decided to steal it? Teddy had gone around boasting about its value. Perhaps he'd made one of them so jealous they'd decided to swipe it.

There was a loud spluttering noise from beneath us as the engine started up again. Laila rushed back in. There was oil all over her hooves and jacket.

"All done now," she said. "Hopefully we can make up for the delay."

She spotted the pile of broken glass that Florence had left, and opened the cupboard to get a dustpan and brush.

As I watched her do it, everything fell into place.

"Got it," I said, turning to Teddy. "Come with me."

I led him down to the lower deck, and knocked on the door of cabin one.

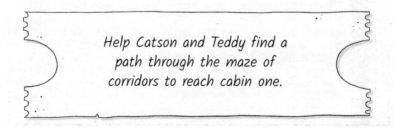

*Help Catson and Teddy find a path through the maze of corridors to reach cabin one.*

START

Florence opened it. Her cabin had a large bed against the left wall, and a writing desk against the back wall. Her cases were piled next to the right wall, and she'd tossed the cup into the middle of them.

"Have you brought my grass salad?" she asked.

Teddy pushed past her and grabbed the cup.

"I'll have that back," he said.

"Finally, someone has come to take my dirty cup away," said Florence. "You can do my laundry next. I would expect quicker service on a luxury cruise."

"I think you have a different idea of luxury from the rest of us," I said. "There are no servants here to wait on you or anyone else. And you can't just take whatever you see lying around. Some things, like that golden cup, belong to others."

We waited at the doorway, expecting some sort of apology.

"Don't be ridiculous!" she said. "And get me my grass salad. I shouldn't have to ask twice."

She slammed the door and we went back up the stairs.

"Thanks for sorting that out," said Teddy. "I'm thinking of selling this cup when I get back home. I can give you a share as a reward if you like."

"Don't worry about it," I said, knowing that the reward would be small, unless he could find someone else as gullible as him.

I took my seat next to Bones again.

"Sounds like that's all solved," he said. "It's a shame, though. I had my hopes up for a more taxing crime."

"Perhaps you'll get one," I said. "Someone's bound to push that hippo overboard eventually."

Laila pulled us up to the shore just after nine o'clock that evening, and we all went back to our cabins to sleep.

By the time I woke up the next morning, we were moving again. I went to the walkway outside the lounge and found Bones and the others staring into the distance. I followed their gaze and saw three triangles rising from the horizon.

These were the Great Pyramids, the only ancient wonders of the animal world still standing.

Can you spot eight differences between the pyramid scene and its reflection in the river?

I had to blink tears from my eyes as I gazed out at the mighty work of the old cats. Thousands of years ago, while the rest of the world hadn't even invented the fetching stick, the felines of Egypt were creating these wondrous structures.

"I wouldn't go anywhere near them," said Walter. "They're bound to have scary mummies inside."

"It just goes to show how far standards have slipped," said Florence. "Those old pharaohs could get their subjects to build those gigantic things, and I can't even get someone to fetch me a decent grass salad."

The others soon drifted away, but I stayed at the side of the boat and watched until the monuments to the great cats were tiny dots on the horizon.

We were getting close to the Valley of the Cats, the resting place of the ancient cat pharaohs, and Walter's mention of mummies had got my fur prickling again. I gripped the pawrail tight as I thought about what might be waiting for us inside the tombs.

But I told myself to take inspiration from the great cat builders of the past. If they could be tough enough to lug huge blocks around in the monstrous desert heat, I could surely be brave enough to peek inside a sarcophagus.

# Chapter Five

Laila brought the boat to a stop in front of a wide, dusty plain with two rows of hills rising in the distance. The Valley of the Cats lay between them, lined with the tombs of the ancient pharaohs.

Laila opened the gate and lowered the wooden gangplank to the shore. The other animals went towards it, but Laila blocked the way and clapped her hooves to get everyone's attention.

"Welcome to the Valley of the Cats," she said. "We'll spend the rest of the day here. It's one o'clock now, and I want everyone back on here and ready to go at six. Okay?"

Laila took her watch out of her satchel and held it up.

"Hold up your watches so I know you've got them," said Laila.

Bones took his watch out of his shirt pocket and held it up. Teddy and Walter held up their wristwatches. Annabelle and Florence tutted and fished around in their bags.

Can you match the character to their watch using the clues below?

- Florence, Walter and Laila all have numbers on their watches.

- Sherlock's watch and Teddy's watch have Roman numerals instead of numbers.

- Teddy's watch has a thick strap.

- Gerald and Annabelle share a watch — their watch doesn't have numbers or Roman numerals on it.

- Florence's watch has a much thinner strap than Walter's.

- Laila has a pocket watch.

A.

B.

"Excellent," said Laila. "So there will be no excuses not to be back here with the rest of the gang."

Laila pointed over to the valley.

"There are twelve empty tombs," she said. "You can explore those as you wish — everything inside was stolen by robbers long ago. But Tutancatmun's tomb is still full of valuable and fragile things, so you'll need to visit that as one group with Ahmet, who's in charge of the site. This is him now."

She pointed to a grey cat in a brown suit who was wandering across the plain. He had round glasses and neat whiskers.

"Greetings!" said Ahmet. "Let me take you to Tutancatmun's tomb right away, while we're all together as a group."

Laila stepped back from the gangway and Florence shoved in front of Teddy. The bison muttered grumpily and went down next. Annabelle and Gerald followed, we went after them, and Walter trailed at the back.

Ahmet led us through the plain and towards the valley. The sun was even hotter than in El Kitten, and I had to keep stopping to sip from my water bottle.

As we approached the first hill, I heard Walter howling behind us.

I wondered if he'd stood on a rock, but when I turned around, I saw he'd curled himself into a ball and was quaking on the floor.

"We can't go in," he said. "We'll be cursed if we look at the pharaoh's mask."

Ahmet adjusted his glasses and strolled back over to Walter.

"There's no curse," said Ahmet. "It's just a silly made-up story. The pharaoh's mask is a wonder to behold."

Walter got back to his feet and took a few trembling steps. But he soon came to a stop again.

"It's no use," he said. "I can't carry on. The rest of you go ahead if you dare, I'll be back on the boat."

He turned and walked back with his shoulders drooping. For a moment, I felt like joining him. At least that way there would be no chance of a mummy coming after me. But I knew Bones would never let me forget my cowardice.

"Strange animal," said Ahmet. "At least that means the tomb won't be too crowded."

We followed a stony path into the valley. The first hill on our left had a narrow entrance carved into it.

"This was the tomb of Queen Neferkitty," said Ahmet. "We found priceless statues, jewels and paintings inside, all of which are now in the El Kitten museum. You can look around these empty tombs for as long as you like after we've visited Tutancatmun's, but please don't use any of the dark corners as a toilet. I shouldn't need to warn you about that, but I had a very rowdy boatload of dogs visit last week."

"If only I'd been there," said Bones, wistfully. "I could have identified the culprit from the shape and smell of their droppings."

The second hill on our right also had a small passageway in the side. This one had a rope tied across it and a 'NO ENTRY' sign.

Ahmet unfastened the rope and beckoned us in.

"Welcome to the final resting place of King Tutancatmun," he said. "Whatever you do, please don't touch anything."

Florence marched in first, with her ears scraping the top of the tunnel and dislodging tiny stones. For a moment, I was worried the whole thing would collapse, and we'd be trapped inside and at the mercy of the mummy.

Teddy, Annabelle and Gerald went next, then Bones and I followed. It was a relief to be out of the sun, even if the air inside was very stuffy.

The tunnel soon opened into a large chamber with a wide stone table in the middle. There was a sarcophagus on top, and I trembled as I imagined an ancient, bandaged cat leaping out.

Lamps had been placed in each corner of the wide space. In the dim light, I could see that Ahmet had arranged dozens of jars, figures and statues along the walls.

Can you pick out the following groups from Ahmet's treasures?

A.

B.

C.

He'd also brushed the dust away from the walls, revealing pictures of ancient cat pharaohs in robes and golden headdresses. Underneath them were rows of hieroglyphics, the picture writing of the old cats.

Opposite the entrance was a huge stone statue of a cat with a long beard, who had its paws folded across its chest.

"You can imagine how I felt when I discovered this place," said Ahmet. "I stepped in and realized I was the first animal to see any of these treasures for thousands of years. Many of the other tombs in this valley had been broken into by thieves before we found them, but here everything was intact, and in perfect condition."

Ahmet paced around the table in the middle.

"Perhaps the legend of the pharaoh's curse helped to keep robbers away all that time," he said. "All the items were in a real jumble at first. I had to spend months carefully untangling—"

Ahmet broke off and gasped.

Over by the back wall, Florence had picked up one of the jars and taken a papyrus scroll out of it.

Ahmet rushed over, yanked the jar out of her grasp and placed it carefully back on the shelf.

"Didn't you hear what I said?" he shouted. "No touching! These fragile artefacts need to be studied by experts. Any slight damage would be a disaster."

"They won't find anything interesting in this one," said Florence, unravelling the scroll. "It's just a load of pictures of eyes and birds."

She tossed the scroll over her shoulder, and Ahmet had to leap to catch it.

"Right!" he yelled, pointing at Florence. "You clearly can't be trusted! Go and stand by the exit until it's time to leave."

Florence plodded over, tutting to herself.

Ahmet carefully rolled the scroll back up and placed it in the jar.

"Where was I?" he asked. "Ah, yes. I sorted through all the items and stacked and numbered them. There were many wondrous finds, but the greatest of all was in here."

He wandered over to the sarcophagus and pulled the heavy stone lid aside.

I prepared myself to spring for the exit if a mummy jumped out. But nothing appeared, so I moved closer.

The pharaoh's golden mask was lying on a bed of old brown cloth. It showed the face of a regal cat with a stripy headdress and a long beard. Coloured glass and precious jewels were set into the gold to create the cat's wide green eyes and the lines of the headdress.

Even in the dim light cast by the lamps above us, it was clear that the mask was an astonishing find. It was almost impossible to believe it had survived unharmed for centuries.

"Behold," whispered Ahmet. "The face of Tutancatmun."

"Wow," said Gerald, gazing at the mask through his sunglasses. "It's pretty cool." These were the first words I'd ever heard the panda say.

I was so entranced by the mask, it took me a while to notice that there was something missing from the sarcophagus.

"Where's the king's mummy?" I asked. "Have you taken it away?"

"No," said Ahmet. "There was no trace of a body in there — just the mask. It was most unusual."

My eyes shot to the dark corners of the tomb in case the mummy had escaped and was waiting to pounce. But I told myself to stop being such a kitten.

"One of the researchers at the museum thinks this might not even be the true resting place of Tutancatmun," said Ahmet. "They say that this was just a decoy sarcophagus to distract thieves from the real one. If so, I can only imagine how grand the genuine one is."

Teddy leaned so close to the mask that I could see his furry face reflected in it.

"You know, I think that mask would look just right in my hallway," he said. "In fact, I'm going to go ahead and make you an offer of one hundred Egyptian pounds right now."

Ahmet glared at him.

"What are you talking about?" he asked.

"I'm trying to make a deal," said Teddy. "And I can see you're playing tough, so I'm just going to come out and raise my offer to two hundred."

"Of course you can't buy it," said Ahmet. "It's priceless. That means you couldn't afford it with all the money in the world. Finding it was the greatest experience in my life, alongside the birth of my kittens, and when it goes on display in our museum, it will fill our whole nation with pride. How on earth could you think it would be for sale?"

Teddy looked up from the mask and stared at Ahmet.

"Alright," he said. "Final offer, three hundred."

Ahmet pushed the sarcophagus lid back in place.

"That's it," he said. "Everybody out. I don't have to share my country's treasures with you silly tourists if I don't want to."

He pointed at the exit and we all traipsed back out into the bright sunlight.

"Tough customer," said Teddy.

Florence, Teddy and the pandas strolled along the path that led deeper into the valley, while Bones and I followed at a distance.

"That was a shame," I said. "We travelled thousands of miles to see the mask, and got kicked out because of the bad behaviour of others."

"Don't worry," said Bones. "I've got an idea. As soon as Ahmet wanders away, we can sneak back on our own and take a proper look."

It seemed like a risk. If Ahmet came back and discovered us, he'd be furious. But we had come a very long way . . .

"Okay," I said. "Let's do it."

# Chapter Six

We split the next couple of hours between exploring the empty tombs and checking to see if Ahmet had left Tutancatmun's unguarded. He seemed to be constantly popping in and out.

The other tombs had drawings of cat kings and picture writing on the walls, too. I asked Bones what they all meant as we wandered around them.

The first tomb showed a cat king on a golden throne, surrounded by his subjects who were walking around on all four paws.

"Only the king could walk on two legs in the royal palace," said Bones, pointing at the picture. "Every other cat had to crawl as a sign of respect."

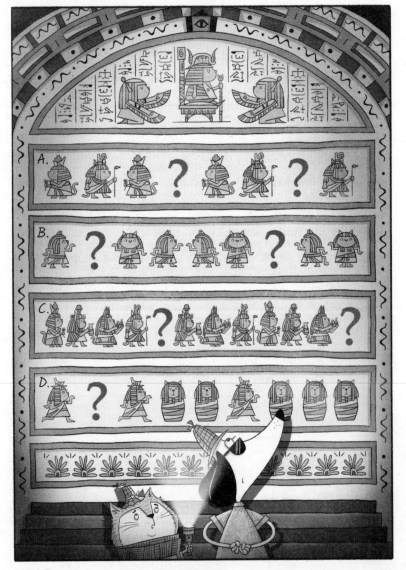

The second tomb showed one of these crawling cats placing small brown circles on a set of scales.

"Those brown dots are ancient cat biscuits," said Bones. "They were made from grain and spices. Every cat in the kingdom had to give twelve to the king each year."

"That's a bit mean," I said. "Did the poor working kitties have to starve while the kings and queens stuffed their faces?"

"At first," said Bones. "But King Tutancatmun came up with a fairer system. He stored the biscuits in a secret room in his palace. Then, if there was a famine, he would hand them out to his loyal subjects."

The third tomb had a triangle etched on the wall. It was split into four strips from top to bottom. Each strip contained different animals. The bottom row showed four dogs, the next showed three birds, the one above showed two cats, both crawling on their paws, and the top one showed a cat in a headdress who was walking on its feet.

"What does this picture mean?" I asked.

Bones growled as he examined it.

"I've read about this. It is called the 'Pyramid of Importance'. It's how the ancient cats thought animals should be ranked," he said. "With kings and queens on the top, then ordinary cats, then birds, then dogs right at the bottom. Let's just say they weren't wise about everything."

We wandered back outside into the bright sunlight.

"Enough about what the old cats believed," he said. "Let's try and get back to that mask."

We peered back towards the entrance of Tutancatmun's tomb. Ahmet was standing outside and examining a scroll.

"Looks like he'll be there all day," I said.

A tall figure was approaching along the path. Ahmet put his scroll down and jogged over to greet them. I shielded my eyes and saw it was Laila.

"Hello," said Bones. "We might be in luck."

Laila pointed over her shoulder and Ahmet nodded. They both went off in the direction of the boat.

"This should give us a few minutes," said Bones.

We raced down the path and went straight back into Tutancatmun's tomb.

It felt bigger and colder now we were alone in it. The cats on the walls seemed to be giving us angry sideways glances, and I was caught between checking the doorway to see if Ahmet was coming and checking the dark corners to see if any mummies were hiding.

"I think I should wait outside and keep watch," I said.

"No need," said Bones. He took his watch out of his shirt pocket. "It's half past three. It would take six minutes for a cat to walk to the boat at the briskest pace. So even if Ahmet comes straight back, we have twelve minutes."

Bones pulled the lid of the sarcophagus aside and we stared in silence at the golden mask. Gazing at it without having to worry about Florence grabbing it or Teddy trying to buy it was much more peaceful. The king's face was as serene as if he'd just finished a bowl of cat biscuits and settled in a patch of sun for a nap.

Can you find the following pieces in this picture of Tutancatmun's mask and work out their co-ordinates?

66

"We've still got a few minutes to look at the rest of this place," said Bones, sliding the lid back.

He paced around the chamber, examining the walls with his magnifying glass.

"Come on," I said. "We've done what we wanted to."

"This is odd," said Bones, tapping the wall next to the giant cat statue. "It feels hollow."

He jogged around to the side of the statue and gave it a shove. It didn't move.

"Help me out," he said.

"Are you crazy?" I asked. "You saw how Ahmet reacted when Florence messed with the jar. How do you think he'll feel if he catches us moving statues around?"

"He won't catch us," said Bones.

I knew there was no point arguing with Bones when he was like this. The quicker I helped him look behind the statue, the quicker we could get out of there.

I joined Bones on the far side and we shoved the statue together. I had to strain all my muscles just to move it a tiny distance along the wall.

"There," said Bones, pointing down to the floor. "Just as I suspected."

There was a small, low tunnel where the base of the statue had been. Bones crouched down and pulled away thick layers of cobwebs so he could look inside.

"Isn't this exciting?" asked Bones. "We're the first animals in thousands of years to see this."

I bent down next to him, and was peering into the gloom when I heard something behind us. Low, shuffling steps were coming down the passage towards the tomb. An image of a stooping figure covered in bandages flashed into my mind and my heart hammered in my chest.

"It's the mummy!" I cried. "It's coming for us."

"No, it isn't," hissed Bones. "But it could be Ahmet, which would leave us with a lot of explaining to do. Let's get in the tunnel. We'll just have to hope he doesn't notice the statue has moved."

Bones launched himself through the cobwebs and I saw his feet disappear into the darkness. I forced myself to go in after him. The dust was so thick, it was like sticking my face in a litter tray.

The steps entered the chamber. There was a grunt, then the sound of stone scraping against stone.

Some of the dust wafted up to my nose. I could feel a sneeze coming, and stuck my paw over my nose to stop it.

It was no use. I sneezed on the floor, sending up a thick cloud of dust that got into my eyes and ears.

The steps came towards us.

"Oh dear," said Bones.

There was a louder scraping noise, this time coming from right behind me. When the dust settled, I turned and saw that the statue had been pushed back over the opening of the tunnel.

"Stop!" I cried. "We're in here!"

I tried to shift the statue aside again, but it was no use. It completely covered the end of the tunnel, with no gap for me to get my paws in. I flipped over on to my back and tried to kick it forward. I didn't care if I broke the precious artefact, I just wanted to get out.

"Ahmet!" I shouted. "Come back!"

The steps hurried out of the tomb.

"I'm not sure that was Ahmet," said Bones. "It took both of us to lift that statue. I doubt he could have moved it on his own."

My chest felt tight, and I struggled to breathe. The walls seemed to become even narrower, as if they were closing in.

"It's no good," I said. "We're trapped!"

"Not quite," said Bones. "This tunnel might lead us to another way out. Let's see."

He crawled onwards into the gloom and I had no choice but to follow.

# Chapter Seven

Bones switched his torch on. The small tunnel had opened into a wide passageway with brick walls, a high ceiling and wide paving stones across the floor.

"Look at all this," said Bones, shining his torch on the wall to our left. He wiped away a thick coating of dust to reveal a painting of a cat sitting on a golden throne. "Ahmet's going to go crazy when we tell him about it."

"If we tell him about it," I said. "We might be stuck in here forever."

The passage went on ahead of us, but I could see no sign of an exit. It seemed to be leading us deep under the hillside.

"Stop worrying," said Bones, stepping forward. "I'm sure we won't be—"

Bones was cut off by a loud twang. He yelped and jumped back, which made me scream, too.

"Hello?" I asked. "Is someone there?"

I could hear nothing but the echo of my own voice.

"Nobody's here," said Bones. "But this is."

He was examining an arrow by the light of his torch.

"It flew out of the wall when I stepped on one of those flagstones," he said, pointing to the ground ahead of us. "It would be in my right leg if I'd been any slower."

I felt as though a snake was coiled around me, squeezing my chest.

"We'll have to go back and keep trying to topple the statue," I said. "We can't go on and risk getting struck by one of those things."

I took my emergency packet of cat biscuits out of my bag. There were fourteen left.

"We barely have enough food to last a day," I said. "What will we do?"

"We can stop panicking for a start," said Bones. "Then we can think clearly. Now let me see . . . This arrow was meant to keep unwanted visitors out. But there must be some way to get across the stones safely."

He swept his torch around the wall to our right, wiping away cobwebs with his free paw.

A few lines of ancient picture writing emerged.

Bones squinted at it.

"Pass three tests to find the king," he read. "First, climb the pyramid."

"Which pyramid?" I asked. "The ground is completely flat."

"Good question," said Bones. He felt the walls with his free paw. "Maybe there's something we press to reveal a secret stairway."

I slumped down to the ground and let out a long sigh. How were we ever going to work out what the clue meant?

In the dim light of Bones' torch, I noticed an odd thing about the paving stones in front of me. They all had something carved into the middle, but I couldn't make out exactly what.

"Bones," I said. "Shine the light down here!"

Bones bent down and pointed his torch at the stones. Small pictures of dogs, birds, and cats on two or four legs had been etched into each one. "Of course!" yapped Bones. "The clue didn't mean an actual pyramid, but the Pyramid of Importance we saw etched into the tomb earlier. So, to climb the pyramid, we just need to remember the order in which the animals went."

ORDER TO FOLLOW:

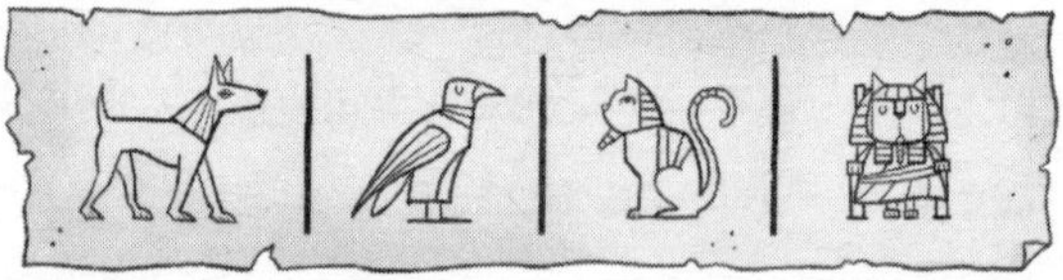

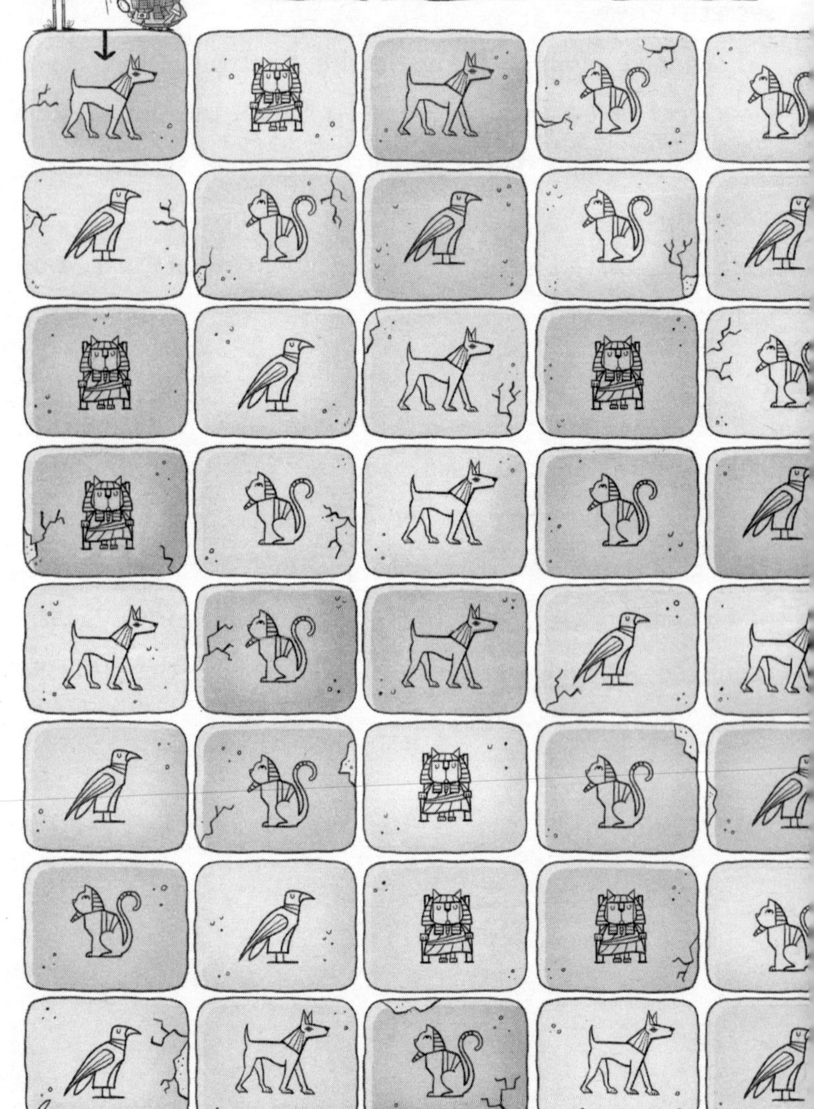

Can you help Bones and Catson get across the floor by following the symbols in the order shown? You can move across, up and down, but not diagonally.

FINISH

He leapt on to a stone with a picture of a dog in the middle.

I covered my eyes, expecting to hear another thwacking sound and see Bones rolling around in agony. But nothing happened.

"Next were birds," he said.

He hopped on to a stone in the next row. Nothing stirred.

"Then came cats on four legs," said Bones, jumping on to a stone in the third row. "Then the cat kings and queens."

He jumped on to the final row, and made it safely across to the far side.

"Simple," he said. "Now your turn."

Bones shone the torch on the correct stones, and I followed the light, bracing myself for an arrow in the thigh.

I leapt right, then right again, then left, and finally made it across.

"Phew," I said, collapsing to my knees. But as I did so, my tail swished on to one of the incorrect stones. An arrow flew just over the top of it, fast enough to shear the fur off.

I sprung forward as quickly as if it had hit me. I could only imagine the pain I'd have felt if the rusty arrow had pierced my skin.

Bones shone his light ahead of us and walked forward very slowly.

"Let's be careful now," he said. "I've a feeling that won't be the tunnel's only nasty surprise."

Bones was right. After a few steps, a deep pit appeared ahead of us. He got down on his chest and shone his torch into the gap.

"Careful," I said. "There could be more of those arrows."

"I don't think so," said Bones. "This is a different test, the second of the three that were mentioned on the wall back there. The danger this time is that we might get stuck in that pit and have no way out."

I crouched next to him and gazed down. I could just about make out a floor, and there were no pawholds on the wall. Even an Olympic pouncing champion couldn't get out of there.

There was a wooden bowl on a copper lever sticking out of the wall to our left.

"Do you think we could leap on to that and make it to the other side?" I asked.

"It doesn't look strong enough," said Bones. "There must be some sort of clue around here."

He got up and scrubbed the wall. Thousands of ancient dust particles danced in the light of his torch.

"Here we are," said Bones, pointing to more hieroglyphics. "It says, 'Present your gift to the king'."

"What gift?" I asked. "Were we meant to bring one?"

Bones turned his torch back to the metal lever and the bowl.

"It looks like part of a set of scales," he said.

I knew I'd seen some scales recently, but it took me a few moments to remember where.

"Like the ones in the painting we saw," I said. "When you told me about how they all had to give biscuits to the king."

"Of course!" said Bones. "It means the gift of twelve cat biscuits, which everyone had to give to the king. If you place twelve cat biscuits in the bowl, we'll be able to cross. You said you had fourteen with you, didn't you?"

"Those are our emergency supplies," I said. "We'll starve without them."

"And we'll be stuck here if you don't use them," said Bones. "Where we'd starve even if we had a bumper pack."

I supposed Bones was right. No one was ever going to rescue us. The only chance of escaping we'd ever have would be to pass the tests.

I took the biscuits out of my bag and stood up. The bowl was about halfway across the pit, and getting the biscuits to land in it wasn't going to be easy.

Bones held his torch out, shining it right at the bowl.

Catson needs to get exactly twelve biscuits into the bowl to cross the pit. Which of the equations on the rocks equals twelve?

I swung my paw back and forth, then released the biscuit.

It landed in the middle of the bowl, but with too much force. It skidded over the side and landed deep in the pit.

"Never mind," said Bones, without taking his eyes from the bowl. "We can afford a couple of mistakes."

I tried again. This time the biscuit flew up in a high arc and landed right in the middle of the bowl. There was a grinding noise as ancient metal cogs turned deep within the wall.

I repeated the same thing over and over without missing. The bowl sunk a little lower each time.

Soon, the biscuits were piled almost to the top, and I was down to two.

"Nearly there," said Bones. He sounded confident, but his paw was shaking slightly, making the light jump around.

I threw the next biscuit, but it bounced off the top of the pile and fell into the pit.

"Sorry," I said.

I took a deep breath. There was just one biscuit left. If I missed, we'd be stuck in the passage forever.

"Come on," said Bones. "You can do this."

I threw the biscuit. It bounced off the others, just as the last one had done. But this time it hit the side of the bowl, and stayed in.

The bowl dipped, and there was a whirring, mechanical sound from the pit. Three stone platforms rose up, billowing a huge cloud of dust. They reached floor level, then immediately started sinking again.

"Quick!" shouted Bones. "Let's go."

He leapt from the first platform to the second. The third was already quite far down by the time he reached it. I followed, pouncing on to the stones as soon as Bones had left them.

The third stone was even further down by the time I got there, but I didn't panic. I crouched into my pounce position, wiggled from side to side, and launched myself into the air. I flew over the edge of the pit and landed on all fours.

Bones helped me up.

"So that was the second test," he said. "I dread to think what the final one's going to be."

# Chapter Eight

We edged along the passageway. Bones swung his torch around, wiping the walls with his other paw.

"Stop!" he yelled. "Don't take another step."

More ancient writing could be seen to our right.

"It says 'You may now approach the king'," said Bones.

"Sounds like there isn't a third test after all," I said, trotting forwards. "We can probably just carry on."

Bones grabbed my scarf and yanked me back.

"Of course there's a third test," he hissed. "And, if I'm right, it's the most fiendish one of all. Do you remember the painting of the king we saw in the third empty tomb?"

I thought back to it. The king had been on his throne, while all the other cats were crawling around on the floor. That was how they greeted the king.

"Of course," I cried. "We need to get down on all four paws!"

We dropped to the ground and shuffled slowly forward. Bones had to use his right elbow to crawl so he could still shine the torch.

It reflected off something in the far distance. As we went on, I could see it was a long golden box.

"The real sarcophagus of Tutancatmun," said Bones. "That's why the mummy was missing from the decoy one Ahmet discovered."

I pulled myself up to get a better look. The paving stone in front of me dipped slightly. There was a groaning, clanking sound, and sharp metal spikes shot out of the walls above us from both sides.

Can you help Bones and Catson get safely through the tunnel by only crawling over stones that have six sides and are next to each other? Start and finish on the black stones.

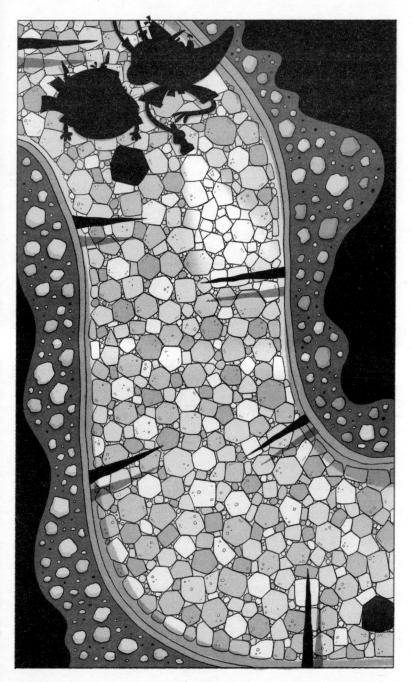

We threw ourselves to the ground. The two sets of spikes came to a stop with their points almost touching. My stomach squirmed as I thought about what would have happened if we'd been caught between them.

"So this is why we needed to crawl," said Bones. "Very clever."

There was a metal screech below us, and the ground rumbled. I felt the stone underneath my right foot fall away, and I whipped my head around. It was murky behind us, but it looked as though the stones we'd just passed over were sinking.

"Looks like there's even more for you to be impressed by now!" I yelled.

I scurried forward, and wondered if I should get up and run, but another set of spikes jolted out of the walls ahead. I had no choice but to keep crawling.

I scrunched my eyes shut and scurried along. I could feel the stones wobbling beneath me like rotten teeth, and hear them collapsing behind me.

Ancient dirt trickled down from the spikes to my fur, but I didn't stop to shake it off. I had to keep going.

Eventually, I felt Bones nudging me on the shoulder.

"You can open your eyes now," he said. "The test is over."

He was pointing his torch at where we'd just been.

The floor behind us was gone, and the spikes were rolling back into the walls.

He span the torch around to show me where we'd ended up. We were in a small, circular chamber. The golden sarcophagus was on a wide slab in the middle, and Bones walked over and examined the intricate carvings of paws and feathers that lined its side.

"You have to admire those ancient Egyptian cats," said Bones. "Look at the detail on this."

"It's hard to admire someone who's just tried to finish you off," I said, getting up and rubbing the dirt from my whiskers.

Bones took out his magnifying glass. The upper half of the sarcophagus had been moulded to look like the body of the king, with his head at the top, his feet sticking up at the bottom, and his paws folded across his chest.

The pharaoh's face looked like a bigger version of the mask that Ahmet had found. It had the same headdress with stripes of blue glass, and the same emerald eyes.

Bones pushed the lid aside, creating a narrow gap. I felt like I should be frightened that the old pharaoh would leap out at us. But after those three traps, I'd run out of fear. An army of undead cats could have jumped out and I would only have shrugged.

The mummy of the king was inside, resting on a blanket of red linen. He was on his back with his paws folded, and was wrapped in layers of bandages that had browned with age.

Now I was finally seeing the mummy, it didn't look scary at all. I felt foolish for letting Hastings and Walter convince me that an old pile of bones and bandages could magically come back to life.

Bones replaced the lid.

"We've found Tutancatmun," I said. "Not that we were really looking for him. A way out would be much more welcome right now."

Bones shone his torch around the walls. We were at a dead end, with no sign of a doorway or passage.

"There must be something," he said.

Starting on our left, he examined every brick of the wall with his magnifying glass. I followed him, blowing at the dust and cobwebs.

I disturbed a spider, who scuttled along and disappeared into a small gap between two of the bricks.

"Look!" I said.

I shoved my paw into the gap and pulled at the brick. A row of bricks spun around to become narrow pawholds, leading up to a dark patch in the ceiling. A tunnel!

Which tunnel will take Bones
and Catson out of the tomb?

"Excellent work, Catson," said Bones.

He clenched his torch between his teeth and we climbed the rungs. They took us through a small gap in the ceiling and into a long, thin shaft.

We kept going for what must have been five minutes, and I didn't want to think about how far down the floor was.

I know that, as a cat, I have no reason to be scared of heights. Cats always land on their paws. My aunt Ruby once fell out of a hot-air balloon and landed safely. But even I felt queasy above a drop that high.

Finally, Bones came to a stop, and I heard something creak open. Bright light filled the tunnel, and it was such a shock that I nearly let go of the rungs.

I scrunched my eyes shut, then looked again. Bones had opened a small, round door, and was climbing out into the sunlight. I followed him, and found we were on the top of one of the hills at the far end of the valley.

We made our way down the winding path. There was a small grey figure waiting for us at the bottom. As we got closer, I could see that it was Ahmet.

"We've got some interesting news for you," said Bones as we approached.

"And I've got some interesting news for you," said Ahmet. "I'm taking you to the police station in El Kitten right now."

He was scowling, his shoulders were pinned back, and his tail was twitching from side to side.

"What for?" Bones asked.

"Because you're going to be arrested," said Ahmet. "For stealing the mask of Tutancatmun."

# Chapter Nine

We walked down the rocky path towards Ahmet, who stepped back from us with his paws up, as if we were dangerous criminals.

"We haven't stolen anything," said Bones. "We're professional detectives. We spend our lives solving crimes, not committing them."

Ahmet pointed back down the valley, towards Tutancatmun's tomb.

"The golden mask has gone missing," he said. "And you were the last animals who were spotted going into the tomb."

"We did go back into Tutancatmun's tomb for another look at the mask," said Bones. "We thought it was unfair that we should miss out because of how others behaved. We moved the big cat statue aside, then hid in a tunnel behind it when we heard someone coming. But that's all we're guilty of."

Ahmet gasped.

"A new tunnel?" he asked. "You must show me at once!"

"All in good time," said Bones. "But first we need to find

out who really stole the mask. Someone came into the tomb and moved the statue back, trapping us in the tunnel. No doubt the same animal made off with the mask."

He rubbed his paws together and grinned. "Well, well, well. It looks as though I have a proper case to crack . . ."

He pelted away down the path as if someone had just thrown a ball ahead of him. I ran after him, and Ahmet struggled to keep up behind us.

When we got back to the boat, we found Teddy, Florence, Annabelle, Gerald, Laila and Walter waiting for us on the walkway of the second deck.

Teddy snorted and stomped his hooves.

"I'm glad you've caught them," he said. "Now let's get them hauled off to jail."

"We didn't take the mask," said Bones. "And I want you all to go into the lounge so I can work out who did."

The animals snorted and grunted, but Ahmet held his paws up to silence them.

"Please do as the dog tells you," he said. "We need to get to the bottom of this."

Bones strode into the lounge and the others shuffled in after him.

I sat on the left, along with Laila, Ahmet, Annabelle and Gerald. Teddy, Florence and Walter sat on the other side. Bones paced up and down the space in the middle, with his paws behind his back.

"It looks as though our little holiday has come to an abrupt end," said Bones. "Not that I'm complaining. I love a good puzzle."

"I'm complaining," said Teddy. "I came here to see the tombs, not to be cooped up in this hot room talking about robberies. I saw you and your cat friend enter the tomb shortly before the mask went missing. How do I know you didn't bury it somewhere and this is all a big act?"

"I don't suppose you do," said Bones. "But you told me that my cases have been reported in your country. So perhaps you'll believe that I've handled plenty of valuable things in the past, and I've always returned them to their rightful owners."

Teddy scowled and folded his arms, but he didn't raise any more objections.

"So," said Bones. "Which one of you took it?"

He gazed at the others one by one. He might have been hoping for one of them to break down and confess, but they all gazed at him in silence.

Teddy glared at Bones and snorted out of his wide nostrils. He'd tried to buy the mask. Could he have decided to steal it when he discovered it wasn't for sale?

Florence held out an empty tea cup to Bones, as if expecting him to refill it. Had she grabbed the mask, still unable to understand that she couldn't just take whatever she wanted, whenever she wanted?

Walter curled himself into a ball and trembled. Was he frightened because the thief was near, or because he himself was the thief and he was scared of getting found out?

Gerald and Annabelle gazed back at Bones, giving away nothing behind their dark glasses. Were they being so mysterious and quiet because they were secretly master criminals in disguise?

Bones even stared at Laila and Ahmet when he came to them. Could they have been secretly planning to steal the mask all along? Had they waited for a group of tourists to turn up so they could pin the blame on them?

I had no idea who was guilty. I was hoping that Bones would point a finger at someone, and say the case was so simple that he couldn't believe I hadn't cracked it. But he just kept pacing around.

"We were trapped inside a tunnel in Tutancatmun's tomb just after half past three," he said. "That will have been when the culprit took the mask. I need each of you, in turn, to tell me exactly what you were doing at that moment."

He took out his notebook and pen, and handed them to me. "Write down absolutely everything," he said.

## Teddy

When we were thrown out of Tutancatmun's tomb by that rude cat over there, I wandered further up the valley to see the other tombs. Just before half past three, I spotted you and your friend sneaking back in. I guess I should have found Ahmet and told him, but I didn't feel like talking to him, so I kept looking at the empty tombs.

### Florence

After we'd finished in Tutancatmun's tomb, I went to look at the other ones. They were a complete disgrace, with no cafés or seats. Call yourself a tourist attraction? I was served a wonderful grass and fern sundae by a charming stoat waiter when I visited the Eiffel Tower last spring. You need to buck your ideas up if you want to compete.

### Annabelle

I was exploring the empty tombs further up the valley.

### Gerald

Yeah. So was I.

### Walter

I was in my cabin, lying on my bed at half past three. I didn't want to enter the tomb at all, and there's no way I would have gone into that terrifying place alone. I just hope that when the mummy comes for whichever one of you stole his mask, he stays away from me.

### Laila

I brought Ahmet back to the boat, and we went up to the wheelhouse so he could talk me through a detailed list of his latest finds. We do this every time I visit, and I take the list back to the El Kitten museum.

### Ahmet

I was with Laila, as she said. Shortly afterwards, I returned to the tomb and found the mask missing.

When all the suspects had given their statements, Bones beckoned me outside. He stood on the walkway and read back over my notes, occasionally breaking off to gaze into the valley.

After a few moments, Ahmet emerged from the lounge and tapped Bones on the shoulder.

"You're not seriously considering me as a suspect, are you?" he asked. "I've dedicated my life to making sure precious artefacts end up in local museums and not in the paws of private collectors."

Bones stared at Ahmet in silence for a moment.

"And what if a collector had made you an offer you couldn't turn down?" he asked. "Wouldn't the best time to take it be when there was a bunch of tourists to frame?"

"What?" asked Ahmet. His tail flicked around behind him. "Of course I would never . . ."

Bones held his paw up to silence him.

"It's fine," he said. "I believe you. I just need to consider every possibility, however unlikely."

Ahmet let out a sigh, and his tail drooped back down.

"Good," he said. "And if you trust me, you must also discount Laila as a suspect. She was with me the whole time."

"Very well," said Bones.

He flipped a few pages back in the notebook and read through my notes again.

"Walter says he was also on the boat at the time," said Bones. "Can you back up his account, too?"

"Let me see . . ." said Ahmet.

He looked up at the wheelhouse and down at the lounge. Teddy was talking to the others inside, but I couldn't hear what he was saying through the glass. I guessed he was taking the opportunity to promote his furdryer range to an audience who couldn't escape.

"Yes," said Ahmet. "As a matter of fact, I can. We were in the wheelhouse when Walter opened the lounge door and asked Laila what the time was. She went down the stairs to look at her watch. It was exactly half past three."

Bones jotted all these extra details in his notebook.

"Very useful," said Bones. "It can't have been him in the tomb either, then. That leaves Teddy, Florence, Annabelle and Gerald. Now let's find out which of them did it."

# Chapter Ten

Bones told everyone to go to their cabins and await questioning, then he got Ahmet to guard the gate to the gangway. We went round all the suspects, starting with Teddy in cabin two.

"Keep a close look at their eyes as I interview them," said Bones. "If any of them have the mask in their cabins, they could cast glances to the hiding place without meaning to."

Bones banged his paw on Teddy's door and we went in.

"We just need to check a few things with you," said Bones.

Teddy was lying on a large bed, which took up the left side of his cabin. There was a desk along the far wall with a chair pushed up to it. Teddy's cases were open, and dozens of different furdryer models were lying around.

How many furdryers can you count in Teddy's cabin?

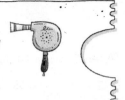

"Aren't you two meant to be the world's greatest detectives?" he asked. "And you're wasting your time on me? Ask anyone from east to west, and they'll tell you the Furdryer King would never need to steal anything."

"You tried to buy the mask from Ahmet," said Bones. "Perhaps you were tempted to take it when he refused?"

Teddy got off the bed and stomped his hooves so hard that the ship bobbed slightly in the water. His black nostrils were flaring and his eyes were fixed on Bones.

"But that wouldn't be a deal," he said, swishing his tail from side to side. "The whole point of making a deal is to get the other animal down to a good price. You can't just take something if you fail. That's no fun."

Teddy looked like he was about to skewer us with his horns, so I ushered Bones out.

"Thank you," I said. "You've been a great help."

We moved along to Florence in cabin one.

She was sitting in a high-backed chair next to the writing desk against the far wall. She'd left all her crumpled blankets and sheets on the floor next to it, expecting a maid to tidy them up.

"I've told you my version of events," she said as we entered. "So make yourself useful and fetch me a bowl of mud. My skin is very dry."

"We won't take up much of your time," said Bones. "We just have a few more questions."

Florence scraped her chair around until she was facing us, took a fan out of her pocket and wafted it in front of her face. I kept a close watch on her eyes, but they didn't flit to anywhere suspicious.

"I didn't steal the mask," she said. "What more do you need to know?"

"We won't be angry if you took it by mistake," said Bones. "Like we weren't cross when you took Teddy's cup. If you give it back now, I'm sure Ahmet will understand."

"Don't be ridiculous," she said. "The mask was completely the wrong size for me. What use would I have for it? Now fetch me that mud. My face isn't going to wash itself."

We thanked her and left. I knew that criminals could be very sneaky liars, but it really seemed as though Teddy and Florence were telling the truth. And neither of them had shot any telling glances at secret hiding places. I hoped we'd have better luck with the final suspects.

We moved on to cabin five and knocked on the door.

"Come in," said Annabelle.

The pandas were lying on a double bed that took up most of the cabin. There was a small desk to the right of it, which had three drawers.

"What do you want?" asked Gerald.

"We just need to check exactly what you were doing this afternoon," said Bones.

"We've already told you," said Annabelle.

"I've got nothing to add to my statement," said Gerald.

It was hard to tell exactly where they were looking with their sunglasses on, but they seemed to be glancing at the desk a lot.

"You must try and help us," said Bones. "You've hardly spoken to anyone on this trip, and you've kept your eyes covered with those dark glasses. It's almost as if you're trying to disguise yourselves."

The pandas said nothing, but I could tell Bones had struck a nerve. Gerald drummed his fingers on the side of the bed, while Annabelle clenched her paws into fists.

Gerald's eyes darted to the bottom drawer of their desk. It was just a tiny movement, but I was sure he'd given himself away. The pandas were the thieves. I was convinced of it.

"You don't seem to be answering the question," I said. "So I will. You're both in disguise because you were planning to steal the mask all along, and you don't want anyone to identify you. And the missing mask is right here."

I strode over to the drawer and pulled it open, confident that I would reveal the mask. But the actual contents turned out to be so strange I could do nothing but stare at them for a moment. They were large photographs of the panda film stars Lily Blossom and Wade Power.

Which of these tiles exactly match the photos of Lily Blossom and Wade Power, and which don't?

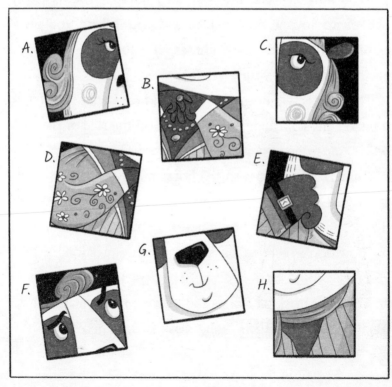

"Do you know these pandas?" I asked, holding the pictures up. "I've read all about them in *Meow!* magazine."

"We don't just know them," said Annabelle, taking her glasses off. "We are them!"

Gerald removed his glasses too, and I gasped. I had been in the company of two of the best-loved pandas in the world, and I hadn't even realized it.

I found myself letting out a loud 'squee!' and clapping my paws. Then I tried to get myself together. The last thing I wanted was to melt down in front of my idols. "I'm sorry I thought you were thieves! I'm a huge fan. I thought you were both brilliant in *The Panda Who Knew Too Much*."

Wade sat up on the bed, sucking his stomach in and squaring his shoulders. He looked much more like the rugged creature I'd seen in all those adventure movies.

"Don't worry about it," he said. "And keep the photos. We always carry them in case we get recognized by fans."

"But please don't tell anyone else who we are," said Lily. "We need to stay in disguise if we want to have a quiet holiday like a couple of ordinary animals, without photographers and reporters swarming around."

"Plus, we don't want that bison on our case," said Wade. "He'll only insist we feature one of his tacky furdryers in our next film."

"You have my word," I said, tucking the photos carefully under my arm.

The picture of Ginger La Marr I'd seen in *Meow!* jumped into my mind, and I couldn't resist the chance to get some inside gossip.

"Just one more thing," I said. "Is Ginger La Marr as glamorous in real life?"

Lily snorted. "Glamorous? She refuses to wear a flea collar, and marks out her territory on set by peeing everywhere. You should be glad you can only see her and not smell her."

I felt my tail droop. I would never be able to watch Ginger in any of her elegant, romantic roles again, without imagining her weeing all over the scenery.

"Thanks anyway," I said.

We trudged out and closed the door.

"I wasn't impressed with your detective skills," said Bones. "As soon as you realized they were famous, you discounted them as suspects. That's how the boxer 'Daddy Bear' Dawson got away with stealing honey for so long, remember?"

"You don't think they actually did it, do you?" I asked. "If Lily Blossom and Wade Power are mask thieves, it's going to be the biggest story of the century."

"No, I don't think they did it," Bones sighed. "But I still have no idea who did. For once, I'm completely stuck."

# Chapter Eleven

We returned to our cabin, and Bones took his rubber bone out of his suitcase and chewed on it. This was always a sign we were dealing with a very tricky case.

I lay back on my bed with my copy of *Meow!* magazine. It just wasn't the same now I knew the truth about Ginger La Marr. What were the other stars like? Did Raven West cough up hairballs between takes? Did Champion the Wonder Monkey fling his poo at the camera operators?

Bones stomped up and down, gnawing the rubber bone so viciously that I thought he would bite a chunk off and swallow it.

He flipped through his notebook, reading my notes over and over again.

After a few minutes, he threw the door open and paced around the deck. I followed him, peering into the small round windows of the cabins. I was hoping to catch a glimpse of one of the animals cradling the mask and chuckling to themselves. But I saw nothing.

All of the cabin windows look the same – apart from one. Can you spot the window that looks slightly different from the rest?

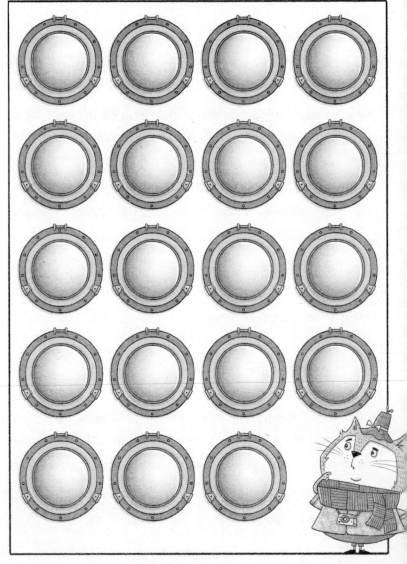

"Getting anywhere?" asked Ahmet as we passed him.

Bones looked like he was about to reply, but he froze and stared at the gate in front of the gangway instead.

"Come with me," he said, beckoning me up the narrow stairs and opening the door of the lounge. There was no one there, but I could hear Laila pottering around in the wheelhouse above.

"Excuse me?" yelled Bones. "Could you let me know what the time is?"

"Of course," said Laila.

She clanked down the metal steps and grabbed her satchel from the top of the cupboard. She fished around inside it, and pulled out her watch.

"It's just gone seven," she said. "We should have left by now. Are you any closer to cracking the case?"

"Yes," said Bones. "As a matter of fact, I think we might be."

He rushed back down to the lower deck and knocked on the door of cabin three.

Walter opened it, stuck his head out, and glanced around.

"Have you found the thief yet?" he asked. "If not, I'd rather keep my door locked."

Bones barged in, pushing Walter back into the room. I followed him, and closed the door behind us.

"Maybe after we've spoken," said Bones.

There was a wide bed on the left of the cabin, and a table with a pile of cases underneath it on the right. Walter jumped on to the bed and cowered behind his paws.

"Don't ask me too many questions," he said. "I don't want to be reminded that I'm trapped on a boat with a villain."

"What exactly did you do after you left the group heading for the tomb?" asked Bones.

Walter peeped out from between his trembling fingers. His eyes shot to the other side of the room, and he seemed to be looking at a battered blue suitcase.

"I came straight back here and locked the door," said Walter. "I thought it would be the best way to protect myself from the mummy."

He glanced over at the bag again, but caught himself, and looked back at us.

"I stayed here the whole time," he said. "Except . . . Hey, wait a minute!"

Walter sat up and pointed upwards, in the direction of the lounge.

"I've just remembered something!" he said. "I went to the lounge to ask Laila the time at half past three. That's when the mask went missing. So I can't possibly have done it."

"It does seem impossible," said Bones. "And yet you managed it."

Walter let his paws fall down to his side. They had stopped trembling. He pulled back his lips to bare his sharp teeth and let out a low growl.

I rushed over to the blue suitcase and unclipped the latches.

I gasped. The golden mask was inside, resting on a black robe.

Walter flipped himself on to his haunches, drew his claws and roared. His sharp white teeth stood out against his black lips.

"Give that to me," he said in a deep voice that was nothing like the unsteady one we'd heard so far.

"Never!" I said. "It belongs in a museum."

I clasped the mask against my chest.

Walter roared and leapt for me.

# Chapter Twelve

I ducked aside, sending Walter crashing on to his cases. He thrashed around in them, crushing one and slashing another.

I looked around for Bones, but he seemed to have disappeared. He hadn't exactly picked the best moment to abandon me.

I scanned the room for somewhere to shelter. There was a gap under the bed that would be too narrow for the lion. I scrabbled under it and pressed myself to the back wall, still cradling the mask.

"You don't want this," I said. "The mummy will come after you, remember?"

"I never believed in any of that nonsense," said Walter. "You didn't really fall for it, did you?"

Walter shoved his paw deep into the gap. His claws missed my face by a whisker. His golden ring was so close that I could make out the staring cat's eye that had been engraved on it.

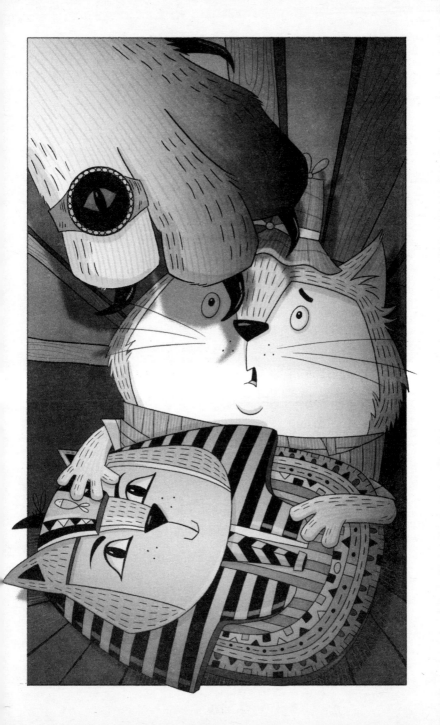

"Give it to me, little kitty," he said. "Don't make me rip this boat apart."

He butted his head against the bed with enough force to make the boat shake. I closed my eyes and braced myself for another attack, but instead I heard a heavy thud.

"Good shot," I heard Bones say.

I opened my eyes. Walter was lying completely still on the floor next to the bed.

"Come out," said Bones. "He can't get you now."

I crawled out, giving Walter a prod on the way just to make sure. There was a large tranquilizer dart sticking out of his right leg.

Laila was standing in the doorway, and Bones was out on the deck, peering around her.

"First time I've ever needed to use one of those," she said, pointing to the dart. "Though I have been tempted by a few difficult passengers. I came close with Florence."

"Well done for holding him off, Catson," said Bones. "By the time he wakes up, the police will be dealing with him."

I stepped out. Laila unhooked a bunch of keys from her belt and locked the door.

Laila has a spare key for each cabin.
Can you match the keys into pairs?

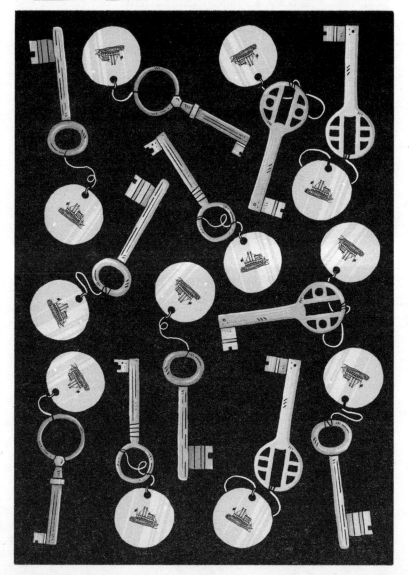

We gathered the others back in the lounge. We took the same places as before, and Bones stood in the middle again.

"Thank you both so much," said Ahmet as I handed the mask over to him. "You will be heroes to our country. But how did you work it out?"

"It was a tricky case," said Bones. "The only suspects who couldn't be accounted for at the time of the robbery were Teddy, Florence, Annabelle and Gerald. I interviewed them all, and but they seemed innocent."

"You got that right," said Teddy, folding his arms. "I would never steal anything. In fact, sometimes my prices are so low, it's like I'm letting customers steal from me. Take the new DeFrizz 2600 model . . ."

Bones held a paw up to silence him, and turned back to Ahmet.

"So that left Walter," said Bones. "The problem was, he could be accounted for. He was on the boat and had asked Laila for the time just before the robbery took place. I turned the problem over and over in my mind, and couldn't come up with a solution. It was only when I saw you at the gate that I had a breakthrough."

Bones pointed out of the window, in the direction of the valley.

"I remembered that Laila had asked us to show our watches before we left the boat," said Bones. "We all did, including Walter. So why did he need to check the time later on? The answer was simple. He didn't. He just needed you and Laila to think he'd been on the boat when the theft took place."

Laila stuck her hoof up and Bones turned to her.

"But he was here," she said. "I saw him with my own eyes at half past three. How can he have been here and in the tomb at the same time?"

"I didn't fully understand it either," said Bones. "Until I tried coming in here to ask you the time. You came down from the wheelhouse to check the watch in your satchel, which you had left unattended. When you told me the time, it was ten minutes earlier than the actual time. That confirmed what I suspected. Before he asked you the time, Walter took your watch from your bag and wound it back by ten minutes."

Laila gasped.

"Here's what I think happened today," said Bones. "Walter made a big show of being too frightened to go into the tomb, ruling himself out as a suspect in the robbery he was secretly planning. When Ahmet came to see you, Walter took his chance to rush out to the tombs and take the mask."

Bones was striding rapidly up and down.

"He was surprised to hear someone in the tunnel," said Bones. "But he thought fast, and moved the cat statue, trapping us inside. If we'd been stuck in there forever, he could have invented a story about us taking the mask and running away. But he still needed to cover himself in case we escaped. So he returned to the ship, took your watch out of your bag and wound it back to half past three, giving himself an alibi for the exact time that the mask was stolen."

Teddy snorted and stomped his hooves.

"And here I was thinking he was too chicken to go anywhere near the tomb," he said. "Well, he had the Furdryer King fooled, and that doesn't happen every day."

"All part of the act," said Bones. "In fact, he played the role so perfectly that it makes me wonder who he really is, and who he's working for. I plan to ask him about it when he's safely in the paws of the police."

Bones turned back to Laila.

"Talking of which, we'd better get going if we want to reach El Kitten by morning," said Bones.

Laila nodded, and climbed the stairs to the wheelhouse.

"I'll stay on here with you," said Ahmet. He tapped the side of the mask. "I need to get this thing safely in the museum before it causes any more trouble."

I heard Laila clanking some levers above us, and soon the boat was rattling along at top speed. It was still only about as fast as a sloth in a traffic jam, and didn't feel like a very urgent way to get a criminal to jail, but at least we were moving.

"That was all very tiring," said Florence, stretching her stumpy legs out. "Now, which of you is going to give me a foot massage?"

We all made our excuses and returned to our cabins.

I woke up as the sun was rising the next morning, and saw that we were pulling into the El Kitten docks. I found Bones peering into the window of Walter's cabin.

"He's still out cold," said Bones. "Let's fetch the police."

Laila lowered the gangplank and we stepped on to the shore.

We were just approaching the police station when a scream echoed out behind us, followed by a loud splash.

We ran back to the boat, and I saw Laila and Ahmet were calling to us from the deck. Ahmet was rubbing his right arm, and there were tears streaming down his cheeks.

"What happened?" I shouted as we approached.

"Walter's gone!" said Laila. She pointed to the cabin behind her. The door had been ripped from its hinges, and there were claw marks in the wood.

"He took the mask again," sobbed Ahmet. His shirt had been shredded and there were scratches on his arm. "I tried to stop him."

Laila pointed to the other bank, where a patch of long grass lead to a row of palm trees, with white buildings rising beyond.

"He went that way!" shouted Laila. "Take this."

She handed Bones a tranquilizer dart, and he shoved it into his bag.

"Come on, Catson," said Bones. "After him!"

Bones leapt into the river and doggy paddled towards the far shore. I took a deep breath and plunged in after him.

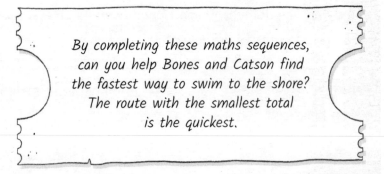

*By completing these maths sequences, can you help Bones and Catson find the fastest way to swim to the shore? The route with the smallest total is the quickest.*

# Chapter Thirteen

Walter's muddy pawprints had led us to a high stone wall that stretched across a whole block of the city. There was a large domed building behind it, and a pair of thick gates halfway along it, with golden handles shaped like cats' eyes.

"That's where he took the mask," said Bones. "But it doesn't look like we'll get far if we simply knock on the door and ask for it back."

At that moment, the gates creaked open, and two cats emerged. They were wearing long black capes, with baggy hoods that cast shadows over their faces, and carrying large cloth bags. A golden cat's eye had been sewn on to the front of their hoods.

"That's the symbol I saw on Walter's ring," I said.

"Indeed," said Bones. "I don't recognize it, and I thought I was an expert in secret symbols."

The hooded cats crossed the road and disappeared into a narrow alleyway.

"Let's see what they're up to," said Bones.

We crossed over to the alleyway and peered around the corner. There were three washing lines stretching across from a small laundry on the left. Giraffe polo necks, mongoose pyjamas and baboon leggings were dangling from them.

The cats left their bags outside the door of the laundry and continued on.

"Excellent," said Bones. "Those might be of use."

He darted down, grabbed one of the bags, and rushed back.

Inside the bag were two black robes. They were identical to the ones the cats were wearing, except that they were crumpled and covered with mud. He threw one at me, and put the other one on over his damp clothes. The robe came to just below his knees, and wasn't the most convincing disguise, but it would have to do.

Can you sort through this pile of smelly washing to work out how many of each of the following items it contains?

Pair of socks    Shirt    Robe    Leggings

I opened mine out, and the smell of stale catfood struck my nostrils.

"I can't wear this," I said, wafting my paw in front of my nose.

"Put it on," hissed Bones. "And be quick!"

I held my breath and wrapped the smelly thing around myself. We crossed back over the road, pulled our hoods down, and knocked on the iron gate. A guard cat, who was also wearing one of the robes, scraped it open.

"Back already?" he asked.

"Yes," said Bones, putting on a gruff voice. "We've already done . . . er . . . that thing we had to do."

We shoved past the guard. He span round and peered at Bones.

"Has your robe got smaller?" he asked.

"That's right," said Bones. "I shouldn't have washed it."

The guard leant forward and sniffed us.

"It doesn't smell like you've washed it," he said.

"I know," said Bones. "I won't be using that laundry again."

The guard gazed at us in confusion, but we hurried away before he could question us further.

The wall enclosed a giant courtyard with a tall domed building at the end. At the front of the building was a heavy wooden door with a golden cat's eye painted on it. There was a large gong bearing the same symbol to the left of it.

We walked down a wide stone path. Groups of cats in black robes were arranged in neat groups on either side of us. Some were wielding wooden swords in perfect time. Others were throwing small metal stars on to circular targets. And others were pouncing on a torch light shone on the ground by an instructor.

"We're surrounded by hundreds of trained fighters," whispered Bones. "If we spot the mask, our only chance will be to grab it and run."

"Who are they?" I asked. "Who's in charge?"

"I have no idea," said Bones. "I thought my *Bumper Book of Secret Criminal Societies* listed every single one, but this is all new to me."

The wooden door opened and another robed cat emerged. He struck the gong three times, and everyone in the courtyard stopped what they were doing. They bowed their heads and trudged over to the domed building in silence.

"Looks like we might be about to find out," said Bones.

We joined a group of cats and walked into the building. There was a stage at the end with three high-backed golden chairs. Above them was a spotlight and two thick wooden poles supporting a banner with hieroglyphics on.

**Decoded message: HAIL TO THE RAT KING**

142

Three hooded figures were sitting on the chairs. One was the size of a cat, one was much smaller, and the other was much bigger.

The golden cat's eye symbol was painted all over the walls, and in a spiralling pattern on the inside of the roof. Looking up at it made me feel dizzy.

The robed cats continued to stream in from the courtyard until we were tightly packed in. Then the door thudded closed behind us.

The large figure and the cat turned to the small figure, threw their arms up, and bowed. All the cats in the audience joined in, and we did the same.

The crowd took up a low chant which sounded like, "Sebkay . . . Senebmiu . . . Yakareb . . ."

"It means the 'The great king has returned'," whispered Bones. "They're convinced the small figure is the living embodiment of King Tutancatmun, and that they'll bring great riches."

"They must be a very stupid bunch," I said.

"It's more likely that they've been brainwashed," said Bones. "Whoever that is in the middle has cleverly wormed their way into their society and got them to worship them."

The large figure took Tutancatmun's mask out from under his robe and held it up to the crowd. They cheered and threw their paws in the air.

The figure threw his hood back to reveal a shaggy mane. It was Walter.

"Just as I suspected," said Bones. "But who are the other two?"

"I have brought the mask back for you, my king," said Walter.

"You have done well," said the small, hooded figure. His voice was high and grating, and I knew I'd heard it before somewhere.

"Let us present it to him," said the cat. He swept his hood back, and I gasped.

It was my old friend, Hastings. Our teachers had always said he'd end up falling in with a bad crowd, but I didn't think it would come to this.

"Of course!" said Bones. "I should have remembered that he had the cat's eye symbol on his medallion. Your old friend has got himself into some very serious trouble."

"This explains why he was so keen to make me believe in the curse," I said. "He wanted to keep us away from the tomb just as much as Walter did."

I felt like the daftest kitten in a litter of idiots. How could I ever have fallen for such a ridiculous fairy tale?

Walter handed the mask to the small figure.

"Excellent," the small figure said. "You have served me well."

I still couldn't place the horrible, high voice. Something about it was making my fur tingle.

The small figure threw his hood back and held the mask above his head. The crowd chanted and bowed again.

For a moment, I couldn't move or speak. What I was looking at seemed impossible.

The small figure on the stage was the most dastardly criminal we had ever encountered. Time and time again, he had turned out to be the evil mastermind behind our toughest cases.

The figure under the hood was Moriratty.

# Chapter Fourteen

Bones growled and pushed his way through the crowd.

"Don't give in to your anger," I said, pulling him back. "Take a moment to think."

"When it comes to Moriratty, we never have a moment," said Bones. "We haven't been this close to him for years. If we don't act now we may never see him again."

Bones was right. Moriratty usually lurked deep in the shadows, while others carried out his foul plans. We'd captured hundreds of his hench-animals without getting so much as a glimpse of him. Now he was right in front of us.

I let Bones go, and he continued shoving his way past the hooded cats.

"What exactly are we going to do?" I asked. "We're surrounded by his devoted followers. They're hardly going to let us take him or the mask without a fight."

"Then we fight," said Bones. "I just need to get a clear shot at him with the tranquilizer dart. If you go up on stage and create a distraction, I might be able to knock him out and take him away in all the confusion."

Even if Bones somehow managed to escape with Moriratty, it would still leave me with three hundred highly trained fighting cats to deal with. It wasn't the smartest plan Bones had ever come up with.

On the other paw, I could see why he was so keen to strike. However slim our chance of capturing Moriratty might be, it could be the only one we ever got.

We reached the front of the stage and Bones pointed to a small set of steps at the side of it.

"Get going!" he hissed.

"Fine," I said. "If I never see you again, it's been nice knowing you."

I took a deep breath and strode up to the stage as if I had every right to be there.

Moriratty scowled and flinched back, grasping the golden mask. Hastings stepped in front of him.

"Hello Hastings," I said. "Fancy seeing you here. What on earth are doing with this strange lot?"

"Get away, Catson," said Hastings. "You don't know what you're getting involved in."

"Oh, but I do," I said, turning to the crowd. "This rat has tricked you all into believing he's a reborn king. But the truth is he's nothing more than a common criminal."

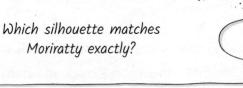

Which silhouette matches
Moriratty exactly?

A loud hiss echoed around the circular space. As one, all the cats threw their hoods back and bore their teeth.

"Don't listen to her!" cried Hastings. "Moriratty is the king we've been waiting for. It was foretold in the prophecy."

"A prophecy which you no doubt faked like those dodgy antiques you sell," I said.

I turned back to the crowd.

"This is my old school friend, Hastings," I said. "He's never been trustworthy. He used to set off clockwork mice in the lunch hall, so he could distract the other kittens and swipe their packed lunches. And now he makes his living by ripping off tourists. He's probably stealing funds from all of you right now, just like his rat friend."

Moriratty pointed his scrawny finger at me.

"Lies!" he cried. "Seize her!"

Walter growled and leapt at me. I jumped aside and he crashed down on to the stage.

"Hurry!" cried Moriratty. "Catch the intruder!"

I climbed up one of the wooden beams and clawed my way into the middle of the banner, swinging wildly back and forth.

Walter roared and pounced at me again. I scuttled rapidly along while he was in the air, and he struck the cloth beside me. His weight brought the banner and the poles crashing down to the stage.

Walter snarled and circled around, tangling himself in the cloth. I landed on the stage, only to see Hastings running at me with his claws drawn.

I could see the dark outline of Bones creeping up the stairs with the tranquilizer dart in his paw. I led Hastings in circles around Moriratty, hoping to keep him distracted.

In my spinning vision, I saw Bones creeping forward. He lifted the dart over his shoulder, but then stopped.

The rat had disappeared.

Walter was back on his feet now, and I had two animals to flee from. I ran in a crazed zigzag around the back of the stage, as they snarled and roared behind me.

I got back to the front of the stage. Bones had apparently vanished, too.

I glanced around the crowd, the walls and ceiling, but I could see no sign of Bones or the rat. It was only when I looked down that I realized where they'd gone.

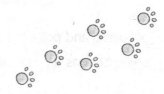

Moriratty had opened a secret trapdoor in the stage, and Bones had followed him down there. Without hesitation, I jumped in, too.

I landed at the start of a dark tunnel that was so narrow I had to drag myself forward with my paws.

There was the sound of heavy padding on the stage above, followed by a loud crunch behind me. I scuttled along, expecting to hear paws pounding after me, but there was nothing.

I looked back and saw Walter. He was jammed at the bottom of the shaft beneath the trap door, with his face and one of his arms wedged in the tunnel.

"Help!" he cried.

"Sorry," I said. "Can't stop now. I hope the mummy doesn't get you."

"You won't escape the Brotherhood of the Golden Eye!" he cried. "We're everywhere."

I continued down the tunnel, ditching my stinky robe and squeezing myself between the narrow sides. It led me to another metal trapdoor, which opened on to the street at the back of the complex.

The block across from me was filled with tall buildings with white walls and arched doorways. There was an alleyway running through the middle, and I glimpsed Bones pelting into it with his dart drawn back and his robe flapping.

I crossed over and followed him in. The houses were crammed tightly together, with the tiny gaps between piled with wooden crates, old bicycle parts and broken furniture.

Another alley appeared on my left, and shortly afterwards, two others appeared on my right. I could hear echoing pawsteps, but I had no idea where they were coming from.

It wasn't hard to see why Moriatty had led Bones in here. It was like a maze, designed to confuse anyone who entered.

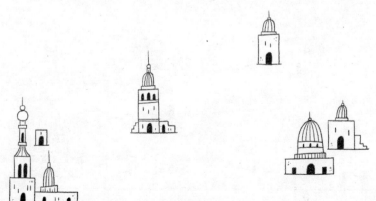

Can you guide Catson through the maze
to catch up with Bones and Moriratty?
Avoid all obstacles on the way.

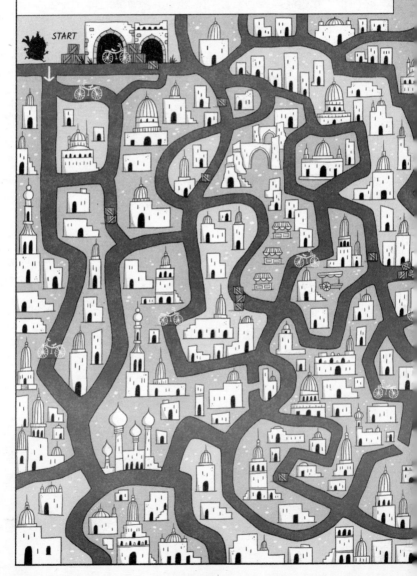

START

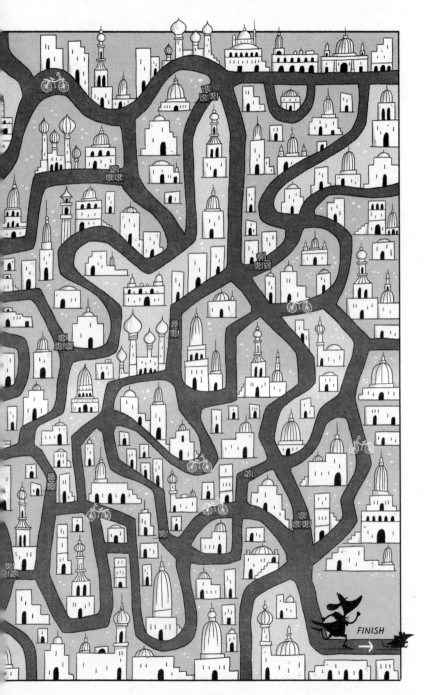

*FINISH*
→

The face of a giraffe appeared at a high window above me.

"Excuse me," I said. "Have you seen a dog chasing a rat around here?"

The giraffe stuck his long hoof out of a lower window and pointed to my left.

"Thanks," I said.

I bolted in that direction, but soon found myself at a junction with another alleyway. I chose left, and raced on, but I had no idea if I was getting any closer to Bones and Moriratty.

I turned left, then right, then left again before finally coming to a stop. There was no point in running if I didn't know where I was going.

I stopped at a junction, struggling to get my breath back, when muffled cries and pawsteps made me look to my right.

For a split second, I saw the rat. Moriratty flitted out of one alleyway and into another. He was still carrying the mask, and it glinted briefly in the sun. Bones ran past a few seconds later, still clutching the dart.

"Stop!" cried Bones.

"Never!" squeaked the rat in his horrible shrill voice.

I ran to where I'd seen them, but by the time I got there, they were gone again. Not knowing what else to do, I jogged back towards the junction. This was the best chance we'd ever had to catch Moriratty, and I was being completely useless.

"Stop!" I heard Bones yell again.

His voice seemed to be coming from the right. It was hard to tell for sure, but it seemed as though they'd looped around and were heading back towards me. I waited at the corner of the junction, ready to jump out at the rat.

I was right. The pawsteps were getting closer. There was the light patter of Moriratty, followed by the deeper stomps of Bones.

The pawsteps got louder and louder. I held off for another second, and then pounced.

One of my paws hit metal. The beastly rat was using the priceless mask to protect himself. Undaunted, I slid my other paw underneath and scooped him up. The mask fell down with a clang.

The rat wriggled free, but I grabbed him again, and this time got both my paws around his waist. I pulled him close to my chest, with his little feet dangling off the ground.

"Let me go," he squealed. "I'll make you pay for this!"

Bones was just a few paces away.

"That's it!" he cried. "Hold him still."

The rat squirmed against me with amazing strength for a creature so small.

Bones pulled the dart back and threw it at Moriratty.

In the second that the dart was flying through the air, two strange things happened. First, Moriratty pushed away from me so violently that he almost pulled me over. I kept hold of him, but had to bend over to do so. Then, I was stung by what felt like the world's largest wasp.

I looked down. The dart was sticking out of my shoulder.

"Whoops!" said Bones. "Just try and hold on to him . . ."

The rat's laughing face wobbled in my vision as I fought the urge to close my eyelids. I told my paws to keep hold of Moriratty, but I could feel my grip getting looser. Bones was so close. I just had keep going for another second.

Everything went dark.

# Chapter Fifteen

At first, I could hear nothing but the mocking laughter of the rat. I was falling into an endless pit while his evil chuckles echoed all around me. Wonky, misshapen mirrors lined the sides of the chasm, and whenever I looked in them, I saw the rat's face instead of my own.

Then I heard another sound. At first it seemed far away, but it got louder until I could make out the words 'wake' and 'up'.

I opened my eyes. Bones was standing over me.

"Sorry about the dart," he said. "Couldn't be helped."

The ground beneath me had somehow turned from hard stone into something very squishy.

My mouth was drier than an Egyptian mummy's armpit, and I had to force my words out.

"The rat . . ." I said. "The rat."

"Safely behind bars," said Bones. "Along with Walter and your old friend Hastings. Despite my little blunder with the dart, you managed to keep hold of Moriratty until I got to him. It was almost a miracle."

I tried to tell Bones that it was nothing really, but all that came out were low murmurs.

"I sat on the slippery little criminal and yelled for help," said Bones. "A local giraffe was good enough to fetch the police. They took Moriratty to jail, and I brought you here."

I propped myself up on my elbows. I was lying in a hospital bed in a small room, with a bright light overhead. Ahmet was standing at the foot of the bed, and I was relieved to see he had the mask back.

"Thanks to you, this is finally going to the museum," he said. "I've told the mayor about it, and she wants to hold a ceremony in your honour."

"No need," I said. "Fighting crime is its own reward."

"She insists," said Ahmet. "Everyone in El Kitten has heard about your heroic deeds, and they all want to thank you."

There were loud hoofsteps in the corridor outside, and an antelope nurse rushed in, scraping her curved horns on the top of the door. Judging from the marks on the doorframe, she'd done this a lot before.

"Leave the patient alone now," she said. "She needs rest."

She took a thermometer out of her top pocket and shoved it into my mouth. Then she shooed Bones and Ahmet away with her hooves.

At noon the next day, Ahmet and Laila lead us to the side

of the market square, where a large wooden stage had been built. Hundreds of cats, dogs, zebras, hyenas and gazelles had gathered in front of it, and I could see Teddy, Florence and the pandas waiting at the side. The pandas had their sunglasses on and were staring at their feet.

Ahmet grabbed our paws and dragged us over to see the mayor, a hairless cat with a huge collar that drooped all the way from her shoulders to her chest. There was a golden medal dangling from it, and it reflected the sun so brightly I had to look away.

"So these are the heroes?" asked the mayor, grabbing my paw and giving it a firm shake. "How lucky we were that the world's greatest detectives happened to be here in our hour of need."

"We were just doing our job," said Bones. He moved closer to the mayor and spoke in a lower voice. "You must promise me that you'll put Moriratty somewhere he'll never escape from. He will need your most secure prison, and your toughest guards."

The mayor laughed and slapped Bones on the back.

"Oh, he'll be well taken care of," she said. "Trust me."

The mayor rushed on to the stage and picked up a megaphone. There was a huge cheer and stomping of hooves from the crowd.

"Thank you all so much for coming," she said. "I'm sure you'll want to join me in thanking these very special animals who came here as tourists, and gave up their time to foil one of the most fiendish crimes our country has ever known."

The crowd barked, howled, roared and clapped. I was about to step on to the stage when Florence and Teddy pushed past.

Florence grabbed the loud speaker from the mayor.

"Will someone get me some grass?" she yelled. "I've been asking for days now."

The applause died down and the locals exchanged confused glances.

Teddy snatched the loud speaker from Florence and stomped around the stage.

"I'm sure you all want to thank Sherlock Bones and Doctor Catson for what they did," he said. "But I've got another important message to share with you all today, which is that you don't have to live with the misery of wet fur. With my new Turbo Dryer 2200, you can be done in two minutes, and that comes with a money-back guarantee . . ."

The audience fell silent as Teddy continued his sales pitch.

I wondered if Bones would rush up on stage and cut him off, but he stayed next to me.

A big crowd has turned out to see Sherlock and Catson meet the mayor. Can you work out which animals are missing from each of the following groups?

Dog    Gazelle    Cat    Zebra    Hyena

"It looks like we're going to miss our moment of glory," I said.

The crowd was dwindling away.

"I've already had mine," said Bones. "It was when I finally got my paws on Moriratty. I don't care what else happens now."

Eventually, the area in front of the stage was empty, though it didn't seem to bother Teddy, who just turned to Florence and continued his speech.

We wandered away with Ahmet and Laila.

"Sorry about that," said Laila. "I shouldn't have invited those two."

"But we really are grateful for what you did," said Ahmet. "Is there anything else we can do for you?"

Bones stopped and stared into the distance.

"There was something," he said. "What was it? Oh, that was it, I'd like you to go and dig up the real sarcophagus of Tutancatmun. We found it at the end of the tunnel behind the cat statue, and we had to pass three deadly tests to get there. It's solid gold, so I think you'll like it."

Ahmet gazed at him with wide eyes and an open mouth. He seemed unable to speak.

"You . . . you mean you found a whole new section of the tomb?" he finally managed. "And you didn't tell me?"

"I've had a lot on my mind," said Bones.

Ahmet grabbed Laila's hoof and steered her in the direction of the docks.

"We need to go back there," he cried. "Right now!"

They jogged away across the square.

"Go in through the trapdoor on top of the hill!" shouted Bones after them. "Otherwise, you might get some nasty surprises!"

The following day, we boarded a large steam ship that would take us back home. Rather than pacing up and down on deck and solving imaginary crimes, Bones was happy to sit back in his deckchair and stare out at the sea. He didn't even look at his books.

I'd never seen him so relaxed before. Sadly, I couldn't say the same about myself.

The previous few days had been a blur, and I kept replaying them in my mind to try and make sense of everything. One small detail kept popping up, and I couldn't be sure if I'd really seen it, so I didn't want to trouble Bones with it.

When we'd met the mayor in the town square, and she'd promised Moriratty would be 'well taken care of', I thought I'd spotted something strange about her collar. There was an image engraved in the middle of the medal hanging from it.

It was a single, staring cat's eye . . .

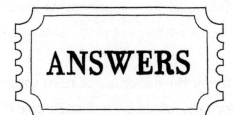

ANSWERS

THANKS FOR HELPING US CRACK THE CASE.

# Chapter One

**Page 9**

**Page 12**

*The items on Sherlock's plate add up to 29*
*(2 + 3 + 3 + 4 + 5 + 6 + 6).*

*The items on Catson's plate add up to 26*
*(1 + 1 + 2 + 3 + 6 + 6 + 7).*

*The items on Hastings' plate add up to 31*
*(1 + 1 + 2 + 3 + 3 + 3 + 5 + 6 + 7).*

*Hastings' meal is the spiciest.*

**Chapter Two**

### Page 18

*Boat F matches the description in the text: it has three levels, a giant paddle wheel at the back and two funnels on top. The lowest deck is taken up with a row of cabins, the second deck has a large covered room and walkway, and the third deck has a wheelhouse for the captain to steer from.*

### Pages 23–24

*1) Four passengers are wearing hats.*
*2) Florence is wearing a necklace.*
*3) False – Gerald is not wearing a flowery shirt.*
*4) Florence has her eyes closed.*
*5) Walter looks nervous.*
*6) Teddy has a moustache.*

**Chapter Three**

## Page 32
*Close-ups A, D and E don't match.*

# Chapter Four

**Page 39**

## Chapter Five

**Pages 46–47**

A = Sherlock
B = Florence
C = Walter

D = Gerald and Annabelle
E = Laila
F = Teddy

**Page 52**

# Chapter Six

**Page 62**

**Page 66**
A. = 3, G
B. = 5, D
C. = 3, B
D. = 7, C
E = 5, F

**Chapter Seven**

**Pages 76–77**

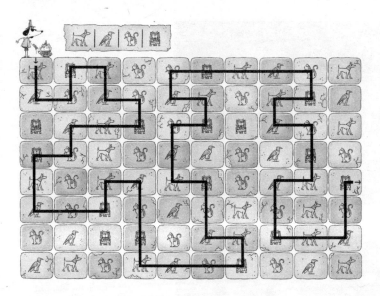

**Page 81**

*The equation that makes a total of 12 is 27 - 15.*

*Here are the answers to the other equations:*

8 x 5 = 40                3 + 7 = 10
66 ÷ 6 = 11              7 x 4 = 28
31 - 16 = 15            100 ÷ 10 = 10
6 + 5 = 11

# Chapter Eight

**Page 87**

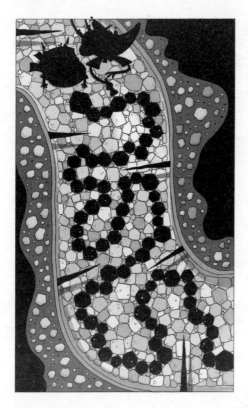

## Chapter Ten

**Page 108**

*There are 25 Furdryers in Teddy's room.*

**Pages 112–113**

*Tiles A, F and H match the photos exactly.*
*Tiles B, C, D, E and G don't match the photos.*

B.

C.

D.

E.

G.

# Chapter Eleven

**Page 120**

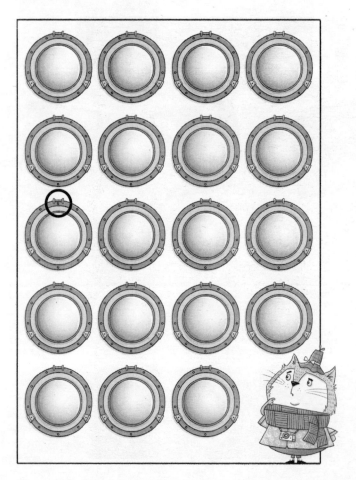

# Chapter Twelve

Page 127

*Route B is the quickest.*

# Chapter Thirteen

**Page 139**
*There are:*
*13 pairs of socks*
*8 shirts*
*2 robes*
*5 leggings*

**Page 142**
*The code says: 'HAIL TO THE RAT KING'*

# Chapter Fourteen

**Page 149**

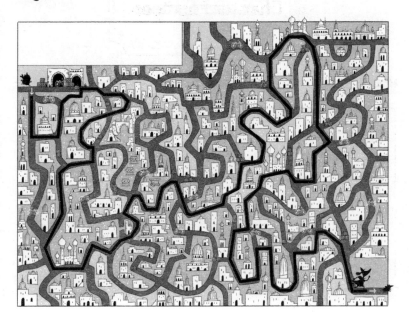

# Chapter Fifteen

**Page 165**

A. Zebra

B. Hyena

C. Dog

D. Gazelle

The End!

# Also available:

**Help Bones and Catson
solve more mysteries in**

*Sherlock Bones and the
Case of the Crown Jewels*

*Sherlock Bones and the
Mystery of the Vanishing Magician*

*Sherlock Bones and the
Horror of the Haunted Castle*

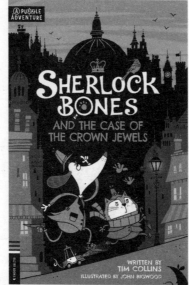

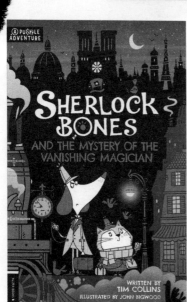

# Publishing in Summer 2024:

## *Sherlock Bones and the Mischief in Manhattan*